"A HOME RUN IN THE MYSTERY FIELD!"
—*Dallas Times Herald*

Generally I don't take my gun to ball games, but that afternoon the Giants were so far behind, I wanted to shoot myself.

Luckily, I found some action in the stands where the curves in the box next to us were more interesting than those on the mound . . .

But just as I was getting to first base, a substitution was made in the line-up, and Wolfe and I were called to the locker room. It seems someone had taken a foul swing at the club's star rookie and smashed his head in with a baseball bat.

THREE MEN OUT

A NERO WOLFE THREESOME

THREE MEN OUT

REX STOUT

*This low-priced Bantam Book
has been completely reset in a type face
designed for easy reading, and was printed
from new plates. It contains the complete
text of the original hard-cover edition.*

THREE MEN OUT

*A Bantam Book / published by arrangement with
The Viking Press, Inc.*

PRINTING HISTORY
Viking edition published March 1954
Dollar Mystery Guild edition published June 1954

Bantam edition / November 1955

2nd printing .. December 1955	*5th printing .... February 1970*
3rd printing .... July 1964	*6th printing ...... January 1976*
4th printing ...... October 1969	*7th printing ...... August 1980*

Acknowledgment is made to AMERICAN MAGAZINE, *in which these
short novels originally appeared.*
*The magazine title for "The Zero Clue" was "Scared to Death";
"Invitation to Murder" was titled "Will to Murder."*

ISBN 0-553-13666-6

Published simultaneously in the United States and Canada

PRINTED IN U.S.A.

16 15 14 13 12 11 10 9 8 7

CONTENTS

Invitation to Murder

1

The neat little man resented it. He was hurt. "No, sir," he protested, "you are wrong. It is not what you called it, sordid familial flimflam. It is perfectly legitimate for me to inquire into anything affecting the disposal of the fortune my father made, is it not?"

Weighing rather less than half as much as Nero Wolfe, he was lost in the red leather chair three steps from the end of Wolfe's desk. Comfortably filling his own outsized chair behind the desk, Wolfe was scowling at the would-be client, Mr. Herman Lewent of New York and Paris. I, at my desk with notebook and pen, was neutral, because it was Friday and I had a weekend date, and if Lewent's job was urgent and we took it, good-by weekend.

Wolfe, as usual when solicited, was torn. He hated to work, but he loved to eat and drink, and his domestic and professional establishment in the old brownstone house on West Thirty-fifth Street, including the orchids in the plant rooms on the roof, had an awful appetite for dollars. The only source of dollars was his income as a private detective, and at that moment, there on his desk near the edge, was a little stack of lettuce with a rubber band around it. Herman Lewent, who had put it there, had stated that it was a thousand dollars.

Nevertheless Wolfe, who hated to work and was torn, demanded, "Why is it legitimate?"

Lewent was small all over. He was slim and short, his hands and feet were tiny, and his features were in scale, with a pinched little mouth that had no room at all for lips. Also he was old enough to have started to shrink some and show creases. Still I would not have called him a squirt. When his quick little gray eyes met yours straight, as they did, you had the feeling that he knew a lot of the answers and could supply good guesses on the ones he hadn't worked out.

He was still resenting Wolfe but holding it in. "I came to you," he said, "because this is a very delicate matter, and the combination you have here, you and Mr. Goodwin, may be able to handle it. So I'm prepared to suffer your rudeness. The inquiry is legitimate because it was my father who made the fortune—in mining, mostly copper mining. My mother died when I was a child, and I never learned how to behave myself. I have never learned, and I am now too old to. A few months ago I had three mistresses, one in Paris, one in Toulouse, and one in Rome, and one of them tried to poison me."

I gave him an eye and decided to believe nothing he said. He just wasn't built for it.

He was proceeding. "I am no longer wild; I'm too old; but I was wild when young. Though my father didn't approve of me and finally refused to see me, he didn't let me starve—in fact, he was fairly generous. But when he died— I was thirty-six then; that was twenty years ago—he left everything to my sister, Beryl, with a request that she consider my needs. She did so, up to a point, until she died a year ago. She was born knowing how to behave, my sister was. I was abroad when she died—I have lived mostly abroad—but of course I flew over for the funeral."

He shrugged like a Frenchman, or anyhow not like an American. "Out of all the millions she had inherited from our father, she left me nothing. Not a cent, not a sou. It all went to her husband, Theodore Huck, with a request that he consider my needs, worded exactly like the request in my father's will. As I said, my sister knew how to behave. I had a talk with Huck and suggested that it would be simpler to transfer a lump sum to me—say a million or even half a million—but he thought not. He said he knew what Beryl's wishes were and felt bound to carry them out, and he agreed to send me the same amount she had been sending the last two years, a thousand dollars a month. I didn't do what I should have done."

He wanted a question, and Wolfe obliged. "What should you have done?"

"I should have killed him. He sat there in his wheelchair —his arteries have gone bad, and he can't walk—he sat there in my father's house, the owner of it, and he said he would send me a thousand a month from the money my father had made. It was an invitation to murder. If I had killed him, with due precaution of course, under my sister's will I would have received for the rest of my life an annual income of some forty thousand dollars. The idea did occur to me, but I'm no good at all with any kind of intricacy, and though I have never learned how to behave, my instinct of self-preservation is damned keen."

He gestured. "That's what brought me here, that instinct. If for any reason this creature, this brother-in-law, this Theodore Huck in a wheelchair, stopped considering my needs, I would shortly die of starvation. I am incapable of sustaining life, even my own—especially my own. So when, at my rooms in Paris, I received a communication warning me of possible danger, I took a plane to New York. My brother-in-law made me welcome at my father's house —damned gracious of him—and I've been there nearly two weeks now, and I'm stumped, and that's why I'm here. There are three—"

He stopped abruptly, aimed the quick little gray eyes at me, sent them back to Wolfe, and said, "This is confidential."

Wolfe nodded. "Things discussed in this room usually are. Your risk, sir."

"Well." He screwed his pinched little mouth, making it even smaller. He shrugged. "Well. I think the warning I got was valid. There are three women in that house with him, besides the cook and maids: the housekeeper, Mrs. Cassie O'Shea, who is a widow; a nurse, Miss Sylvia Marcy; and a so-called secretary, Miss Dorothy Riff. They're all after him, and I think one of them is getting him, but I don't know which one and I can't find out. The trouble is, I have developed a formula for getting on terms with women, but in this case I can't use it and I'm lost. I need to know as soon as possible which one of those women is landing my brother-in-law."

Wolfe snorted. "So you can intervene? With your formula?"

"Good God, no." Lewent was shocked. "It would be a damned nuisance, and anyway there would soon be another one and I would have time for nothing else. Also I would like to get back to Europe before the holidays. I merely want to engage her sympathetic interest. I want to secure her friendship. I want to make absolutely certain that she will be permanently well disposed toward me after she lands Huck. That will take me three weeks if it is Miss Marcy or Miss Riff, four if it is Mrs. O'Shea. It is not a sordid familial flimflam. It's a perfectly legitimate inquiry. Isn't it?"

"I suppose so," Wolfe conceded. "But it's fantastic."

"Not at all. It's practical and damned sensible. My income for the rest of my life depends entirely on the goodwill of my brother-in-law. If he marries, especially if he marries a woman considerably younger than he is, how long will his goodwill last—twelve thousand dollars' worth, year after year—if his wife hasn't got it too?"

Wolfe grunted. "What precisely would be my engagement?"

"To find out as soon as possible which one of them is hooking him." Lewent aimed a thumb at the little stack he had put on Wolfe's desk. "That thousand dollars is yours, succeed or fail, but it will have to cover everything because it's all I can afford. It might seem hardly worth your while, but actually, since you never leave this house on business, it will take little of your time and talent. The work will be done by Mr. Goodwin, and you have to pay his salary anyhow, and the expense will be negligible—taxi fares to and from my father's house on Sixty-ninth Street, now owned by Theodore Huck. I know something of Goodwin's record and prowess, and one trip, one day, might be all he would require—with consultation with you, of course. He can go up there with me now."

I didn't throw him a kiss. I can take a compliment raw,

with no chaser, as well as the next one, but I hope I have learned how to behave, and I had a weekend date.

Wolfe's scowl had deteriorated to a mild frown. "You say you received a warning. From whom?"

"From Paul Thayer, Huck's nephew. Huck lets him live there in the house. He's as useless as I am—he composes music that no one will listen to. He hopes to inherit some of my father's money from Huck, and he got alarmed and wrote me."

"What alarmed him?"

"Some little things and one big thing. A man with cases came from Tiffany's and was with Huck in his study for nearly an hour. That could mean only one thing: Huck was buying something expensive for a woman—one of those three."

"Why? There are other women."

Lewent shook his head. "Not for Huck. He can't walk, and he hasn't been out of the house more than two or three times since my sister died. No woman ever comes to see him. It's one of those three. You might think Paul or I could discover which one, but it's not so simple. He has his meals in his room or his study, and we see very little of him. Paul has tried approaching the women on it, and I have made a few little efforts in that direction myself, but it's a delicate business."

"Make friends with all three of them."

"It couldn't be done. They're too jealous of one another."

"Wait until you see one of them wearing the gift from Tiffany's. That will settle it."

"It would settle me too. It would be too damned obvious. None of them is a numskull."

"But," Wolfe objected, "it will be equally obvious if she is flushed by Mr. Goodwin—in consultation with me."

"I don't expect him to flush her. I don't want him to." Lewent slid forward on the smooth leather seat. "My God, can't you find out things without people knowing it? I couldn't take Goodwin into that house to cross-examine them about their relations with Huck, even if I wanted to. It is my father's house, but Huck owns it. We'll have to use a subterfuge, especially for Goodwin to talk with Huck. I just decided—"

He was stopped by a noise from Wolfe—an explosive noise, half grunt and half snort. It was meant for a stopper. Lewent's quick little gray eyes widened in startled inquiry. "What's the matter?"

"You." Wolfe was mildly disgusted. "I might conceivably engage to pry into the amatory designs of a wealthy widower if I were hard put and the bait was spectacular, but as it is you're wasting your time. And mine. Good day, sir."

It sounded positively final. Lewent's pinched little mouth worked from side to side and up and down. "You mean you won't do it."

"That's right."

"I didn't think you would, but I thought I'd try it that way." He clasped his hands together. "So here goes. Now this is confidential."

"You said that before."

"I know I did, but this is different. My sister died here in New York, at my father's house, of ptomaine poisoning from something she ate. Huck cabled me in Paris, and I flew home for the funeral, as I said. I never had any suspicions about it until two things happened. First, Odelette, my mistress in Toulouse, tried to poison me when she was mad with jealousy, showing me that anyone may commit murder if the motive is good enough; and second, I was warned by Paul Thayer that Huck was being bagged by one of these women. That started me thinking, and I went to a library and read up on ptomaines. Those women were all present when my sister was poisoned. I believe that one of them murdered her."

"On what evidence?"

"None. I believe that she already had Huck or was sure she could get him. I've been here nearly two weeks, and I firmly believe that, but what can I do? I don't even dare ask any questions of anyone. Of course the police would laugh at me. Naturally I thought of you, but the most I could scrape up was a thousand dollars, and that's small change for you, so I decided to try to get you started on it by not mentioning murder and just saying what I wanted—well, you heard me."

He gestured. "I want to head her off, and I think maybe I can if I can find out which one it is."

"How will you head her off without evidence?"

"That's up to me. Leave that to me, if once I know her. For an absolutely legitimate purpose, I want to pay in advance for a thousand dollars' worth of Goodwin's time and talent and consultation with you as required. Ten hours of Goodwin and ten minutes of you? Whatever it is, I want to buy it."

Abruptly Wolfe rolled his chair back and arose. "I have an important phone call to make," he told Lewent, "and will leave you with Mr. Goodwin. Since, as you say, the work will be done by him, I won't be needed, even for the decision whether to take the job."

He marched across to the door to the hall and was gone, but not, as I knew, to make a phone call. Not wanting to refuse to take money, but not caring to shoulder the blame for spoiling my weekend for the sake of a measly grand, he was putting it up to me. As for him, he would go to the kitchen, open a bottle of beer, and make suggestions to Fritz about preparations for lunch. As for me, I was stuck. If I shooed Lewent out it would be months before I could again open my trap to ride Wolfe for turning down jobs. So I got the little stack which the little man had put on Wolfe's desk, counted it, and found that it was twenty fifties.

"Okay," I told him, "I'll give you a receipt. First I think our approach to Huck will stand some discussion. Do you agree?"

He did, and I sat, and we discussed.

2

Lewent's father's house of granite, on Sixty-ninth Street between Fifth and Madison, had apparently not had its face washed since little Herman had been born there back in the nineteenth century, but inside there had unquestionably been changes. For one thing, the self-service elevator was so modern and so large that I guessed it had been installed since the present owner had been condemned to a wheelchair on account of his bum arteries.

Though Lewent had insisted that we should delay the operation until Theodore Huck's lunch hour was past, and therefore it was after two o'clock when we arrived and were let in by a female viking who could have carried Herman around in her apron, I was still nursing the hope that I might earn the grand that day and evening and have my weekend. So when the viqueen had taken our hats I wasted no time for a glance at the luxuries of the big entrance hall as Lewent led the way to the elevator. We left it one flight up and turned right down the hall, which was some narrower but longer than the one downstairs. I was surprised at the thickness of the rugs in a mansion whose master did all his moving in a wheelchair.

The surprise left when we entered a large high-ceilinged room at the rear of the house and I saw the wheelchair. He could have parked it in a trailer camp and lived in it if it had had a roof. The seat was roomy enough for Nero Wolfe. At the sides were shelves, trays and compartments. A large metal box at the rear, low, was presumably a motor housing. A fluorescent light was attached to the frame at Huck's left, shining on a magazine Huck was reading.

Lewent said, "This is Mr. Goodwin, as I phoned you," and turned and went.

Theodore Huck said nothing. Tossing the magazine on a table nearby, he pressed a button, and the footrest of the chair came up, smoothly, until his legs, which were under a large plaid shawl, were straight and horizontal. He pressed another button, and the chair's back receded until he was half reclining. He pressed another button, and the part of his legs were on began to move from side to side, not very gently. He closed his eyes. I lowered myself onto a chair and did a sweeping take of the room, which was his study, with the parts of the wall left visible by pictures and rows of books showing old wood panels, and then went back to him. The upper half of him was perfectly presentable for a guy his age, with a discernible waistline, good broad shoulders, a face with all features in proportion and correctly placed, and his full share of hair that had been dark but was now mostly gray. I had plenty of time to take him in, for he stayed put for a good five minutes, with his legs going from side to side on the moving frame. Finally the motion stopped, he pressed buttons, his legs went down and his torso up, and he reached to pull the edge of the plaid shawl above his hips.

He looked at me, but I couldn't meet him because he seemed to be focusing about a foot below my chin. "I do that sixteen times a day," he said. "Every hour while I'm awake. It helps a little. A year ago I could barely stand, and now I can take five or six steps. Your name's Goodwin?"

"Right."

"My brother-in-law said you wanted to see me."

I nodded. "That's not strictly accurate, but it will do. He wanted me to see you. My name's Archie Goodwin, and I work for Nero Wolfe, the detective, and your—"

"Oh! You're that Goodwin?"

"Right. Your brother-in-law called at Mr. Wolfe's office today and wanted to engage his services. He says that his sister—"

A door off to the right opened, and a young woman my age came stepping in, with papers in her hands. She was fair, with gray-green eyes, and as a spectacle there wasn't a thing wrong with her, at a glance. Halfway across to the wheelchair she stopped and inquired, "Will you sign the letters now, Mr. Huck?"

"Later, Miss Riff." He was a little crisp. "Later will do."

"You said—I thought perhaps—"

"There's no hurry."

"Very well. I'm sorry if I interrupted."

She turned and was gone, closing the door behind her so gently that there was no noise at all. I asked Huck, "That was Dorothy Riff?"

"Yes. Why?"

"I was telling you. Mr. Lewent says his sister promised him that in case of her death he would get a substantial sum. That was about a year before she died, and he is certain she would not have failed to arrange to keep her promise."

Huck was shaking his head. "He heard her will read, and he saw it."

"He says she told him she wouldn't put it in her will because that would have violated a promise she had made her father. He thinks she left it in someone's care for him —not you, he says, for you would have followed her instructions fully and promptly. He suspects it was Miss Riff or Miss Marcy or Mrs. O'Shea, and he wants Mr. Wolfe to investigate the matter, but he says it can be investigated only with your knowledge and consent, and that's why he asked you to see me. Also Mr. Wolfe thought—"

Another door swung open, this time the one by which Lewent and I had entered from the hall, and another female was with us. On a guess she was somewhat younger than Dorothy Riff, but it was hard to tell with her nurse's uniform setting off her big dark eyes and dark brown hair. Stopping for no questions, she crossed to a cabinet, got out a glass, a thermos carafe, and a bottle of Solway's twenty-year liqueur striped-label scotch, put on ounce from the bottle and two ounces from the carafe into the glass, no ice, and went and handed it to Huck and got thanked.

She asked him in a low, cooing voice, "Everything under control?"

"Fine."

"Your two-thirty exercise?"

"Of course."

She left us, having given me just one swift glance. When the door was closed again Huck spoke. "This is medicine for me every two hours, but will you have some?"

"No, thanks. That was Sylvia Marcy?"

"Yes. You were saying that Mr. Wolfe thought—"

I resumed. "He thought that before I talk with the three women—with your permission, of course—you might be willing to let us have your opinion on a few points. For instance, do you think it likely that your wife made some such arrangement as Mr. Lewent suspects? Can you recall ever hearing her say anything hinting at such a thing? Her accounts for the months before she died—say a year—do they show a withdrawal of any unusual amount, either cash or securities? And most important, Mr. Wolfe thinks, which of those three women would your wife have been most likely to choose for such a purpose?"

Huck may have thought he was looking straight at me, but if so his aim was still low. "My brother-in-law has never mentioned this to me," he said stiffly.

I nodded. "He says he was afraid of offending you. But now, since a year has passed and it is evident that all you have for him is the request in your wife's will that his needs be considered, he feels that the matter should be looked into, so far as it can be without any inconvenience or embarrassment to you."

"How could it embarrass me?"

"I don't know. You're a very wealthy man, and Miss Riff and Miss Marcy and Mrs. O'Shea work for you and live in your house, and I suppose Mr. Lewent thought you might not like my asking them an assortment of leading questions."

"Miss Riff doesn't live here."

"The other two do?"

"Yes."

"Do you regard them all as upright and trustworthy?"

"Yes."

"This might help. Are you yourself so certain of the character of any one of them that you would eliminate her entirely from consideration in a matter of this kind?"

He twisted and stretched an arm to put his medicine glass on the table, and, turning back to me, was opening his mouth to reply when the door to the hall opened again and we had another visitor. This time I wasn't sure. There had been no question about the secretary or nurse the moment they appeared, but I had not expected to see the housekeeper in a gay figured dress, white and two shades of blue. Also, though she was a little farther along than the other two, she was by no means a crone. She had medium brown hair and deep blue eyes, and there was a faint touch of hip-swinging in her walk. She came as for a purpose, straight to the front of the wheelchair, bent over from the hips, and tucked in the edge of the shawl around Huck's feet. I watched Huck's eyes. They went to her, naturally, but they seemed more preoccupied than pleased.

She straightened up and spoke. "All right, sir?"

"Yes, thank you, Mrs. O'Shea."

"Any orders?"

"No, nothing."

She wheeled a quarter-turn to face me, and did a take. Her look was too brief to be called deliberate, but there sure was nothing furtive about it. I thought I might as well let her have a grin, but before my muscles reacted to deliver it she was through and was on her way. From the rear the hip-swing was more perceptible than from the front. As I viewed it I reflected that they had certainly wasted no time in giving a stranger a once-over. Entering and ascending with Lewent, I had had sight, sound, or smell of none of them, but now all three had galloped in before I had been with Huck more than fifteen minutes. If they were too jealous for a mutual intelligence pact it must have been radar.

When the door was shut again Huck spoke. "You asked some questions. I think it very unlikely that my wife made any such arrangement as you describe. She certainly never hinted at it to me. As far as I know, during the last year of her life she made no withdrawal of cash or securities not accounted for, but I'll be glad to tell the accountants to check it. Although I do not accuse my brother-in-law of fabrication, I strongly suspect that he grossly misunderstood something my wife said to him. However, since he has consulted Nero Wolfe and you are here, I'm willing to humor him, the poor devil. Do you want to see them separately or together?"

"Together for a start."

"How long will it take? You'll finish today?"

"I hope to. I want to, but I don't know."

He regarded me, started to say something, decided not to, and pressed a button. Instantly the shebang leaped forward like a bronco out of a chute, missing my feet by maybe eight inches with one of its big balloon tires as it swept by. Huck was steering with a lever. Stopping beside the door to the hall, he reached for the knob and pulled the door wide, and the chair circled and passed through. I was on my feet and following when his bellow came.

"Herman! Come down here!"

I know now what had put the whole household on the alert—Paul Thayer, Huck's nephew, had let it out that I was Nero Wolfe's Archie Goodwin—but I didn't know then, and it was a little spectacular to see them coming at us from all directions—Dorothy Riff from a door on that floor, Mrs. O'Shea up the stairs from below, and Lewent and Sylvia Marcy down the stairs from above—none of them bothering with the elevator. They stopped flurrying when they saw Huck sitting composed in his chair and me standing beside him at graceful ease, and approached in no apparent agitation.

Lewent standing was exactly the same height as Huck sitting. He asked as he came, "You want me, Theodore?"

The girls were closing in.

"Yes, I do," Huck told his brother-in-law. "Mr. Goodwin has described the situation to me, and I want you to hear what I say to Mrs. O'Shea and Miss Marcy and Miss Riff." His eyes moved to his womenfolk. "I suppose you have heard of a private detective named Nero Wolfe. Mr. Lewent went to see him this morning and engaged him to investigate something, and he has sent Mr. Goodwin here to make inquiries. Mr. Goodwin wishes to question you three ladies. You will answer at your discretion, as you please and think proper. That's all I have to say. I want to make it clear that I am imposing no restriction on what Mr. Goodwin asks or what you answer, but I also wish you to understand that this is a private inquiry instigated by Mr. Lewent, and you are free to judge for yourselves what is fitting and relevant."

I didn't care for it a bit. You might have thought he knew what I was there for and was making damn sure I wouldn't get it. Not by a flicker of an eyelash had he given any ground for a decent guess as to which one had him hooked.

3

They took me up in the elevator, two flights, to a room they called the sewing room. The name must have been a carry-over from bygone days, as there was no sign of sewing equipment or supplies in sight. Mrs. O'Shea was going to seat us around a table, but I wanted it more informal and got it staged with her and me in easy chairs facing a couch on which the other two were comfortable against cushions.

They were good listeners all right. I took my time about getting to the point, since there was no question about having my audience. I told of Lewent's coming to Wolfe's office. I touched upon his childhood and young manhood, with no mother, not making it actually maudlin. I admitted he had been irresponsible. I told of his having been left out of his father's will. Miss Riff's gray-green eyes, and Miss Marcy's dark eyes, and Mrs. O'Shea's deep blue ones, all concentrated on me, were pleasantly stimulating and made me rather eloquent but not fancy. I told of the promise Lewent's sister had made him a year before her death—

which was, of course, pure invention—of his conviction that she had kept it, and his suspicion that a substantial sum in cash or securities had been entrusted by her to someone to be given to him. I added that he thought it possible that the trustee was one of the women there present, and would they mind answering a few questions?

Mrs. O'Shea stated that Lewent was a frightful little shrimp. Miss Marcy said it was utterly ridiculous. Miss Riff, with her nose turned up, asked, "Why a few questions? You can ask us one, did Mrs. Huck give any of us anything to give to her brother, and we say no, and that settles it."

"It does for you," I conceded. "But as Mr. Huck told you, I'm here to investigate, and that's no way to do it. For instance, what if I were investigating something really tough, like a suspicion of murder? What if Lewent suspected that one of you poisoned his sister so you could marry Huck?"

"That's more like it," Miss Marcy said approvingly, with the coo still in her voice.

"Yeah. But then what? I ask if you did it, and you say no, and that settles it? Hardly. I ask plenty, about your relations with Mr. and Mrs. Huck and one another, and about your movements and what you saw and heard, not only the day she died, but a week, a month, a year. You can answer or refuse to answer. If you answer, I check you. If you refuse, I check you double."

"Ask me something," Miss Marcy offered.

"To be suspected of murder," Miss Riff declared, "would at least be exciting. But a thing like this, and from Herman Lewent—" She shivered elegantly. "No, really."

"Okay." I was sociable. "But don't think I'm not going to grill you, because that's what I came for. First, though, I'd like to have your reaction to a little idea of my own. It seems to me that if Mrs. Huck wanted to leave something for her brother like that, the logical person for her to leave it with would have been her husband. Lewent is sure she didn't, because he says Huck is an honest man and would have turned it over. Which may satisfy Lewent, but not me. Huck could be entirely too honest. He could figure that in leaving a gob of dough for her brother his wife was ignoring her father's wishes, and that was wrong, and he wouldn't go through with it. I think that's quite possible, but you ladies know him better than I do. What kind of a man is he? Do you think he might do that?"

No reply. Nor was there any exchange of glances. I insisted, "What do you think, Mrs. O'Shea?"

She shook her head, with a corner of her mouth turned up. "That's no kind of question to ask."

"We work for Mr. Huck, you know," Sylvia Marcy cooed.

"He's a very fine man," Dorothy Riff declared. "Very, very fine. That's why one of us poisoned Mrs. Huck so she could marry him. What is she waiting for? It's been a year."

I upturned a palm. "That's only common sense. You have to watch your step on a thing like that, and besides, that might not have been the motive. In fact, here's one I like better: Mrs. Huck handed her a real bundle, say a hundred grand, to be given to Lewent if and when Mrs. Huck died. But as the months went by and Mrs. Huck stayed perfectly healthy, good for another twenty or thirty years, our heroine got impatient and acted. Of course she is now in a pickle. She has the hundred grand, but even after a year has passed she doesn't dare to start spending it."

Mrs. O'Shea permitted herself a refined snort. "It wouldn't surprise me if that Lewent creature actually believed that rot." Her tone was chilly, and her deep blue eyes were far from warm. "Mr. Huck said you would ask us question and we would answer as we please and think proper. Go ahead."

I stuck with them for an hour. I have had chores that were far more disagreeable, but none less fruitful. There were assorted indications that there was no love lost among them, and various hints that Huck was not regarded solely as a source of wages by any of them, but to pick one for Lewent at the end of the hour I would have had to use eeny, meeny, miny, mo. I was disappointed in me. Deciding that I had made a mistake to bunch them, I arose, thanked them for their patience and co-operation, said that I would like to talk with each of them singly a little later, asked where I would be apt to find Lewent, and was told that his room was on the floor below us, two flights up from the ground and one up from Huck's study. Sylvia Marcy offered to show me and preceded me out and down the stairs. She had cooed throughout. It was a pleasant and

even a musical coo, but what the hell. If I had been, like
Huck, exposed to it continually, after a couple of days I
would either have canned her or sent for a justice of the
peace to perform a ceremony.

To my knock Lewent opened the door of his room and
invited me in. For the first four paces his room was only a
narrow hall, as rooms frequently are in big old houses
where bathrooms have been added later, but then it
widened to a spacious chamber. He asked me to sit, but I
declined, saying I had had a warming-up session with the
suspects and would like to meet Paul Thayer, Huck's
nephew, if he was available. He said he would see, and left
the room, me following, mounted two flights of stairs,
which put us on the floor above the sewing room, and went
down a hall and knocked on a door. A voice within told us
to enter.

The room was comparatively small, and no inch was
being wasted. There was a single bed, a grand piano, two
small chairs, and a few tons of books and portfolios on
shelves and tables and stacked on the floor. Thayer, who
was about my age and built like a bull, thought he would
bust my knuckles as we shook, and then decided not to
when I reacted. I had told Lewent on the way up that it
might be better if I had Thayer to myself, and he had
agreed, so he left us. Thayer flopped on the bed, and I
took a chair.

"You sure have bitched it up," he stated.

"Yeah? How?"

He waved a hand. "Do you know anything about music?"

"No."

"Then I won't put it in musical terms. Your idea of bust-
ing in with the fantasy of one of them sequestering a bale
of kale intended for Lewent is sublimely cuckoo."

"That's a pity. I offered it as a substitute for Lewent's
fantasy of one of them poisoning your aunt."

He threw his head back and haw-hawed. He was chock
full of gusto. When he could speak he said, "Not my aunt
really—yes, I suppose she was, since my Uncle Theodore
married her. She died in great pain, and I was strongly
affected by it. I couldn't eat properly for weeks. But the
idea of one of those gals giving her poison—absolutely, you
know, Herman the Midget is an imp of prodigious fancy!

Dear God, such witless malice! Nevertheless, I am his staunch ally. He and I are one. Would you like to know how ardently I covet a few of the Lewent millions, now in the grasp of my Uncle Theodore?"

I told him I would love to, but he didn't hear me. He bounced to his feet, strode to the piano bench and sat, held his hands poised above the keyboard with the fingers spread, and tilted his head back with his eyes closed. Suddenly down his hands went, both to his left, and the air was split with a clap of thunder. Other claps and rumblings followed; then his hands started working their way to the right, and there was screeching and squealing. Abruptly it stopped, and he whirled to face me.

"That's how I covet that money. That's how I feel."

"Bad," I said emphatically.

"Don't I know it. Say I had five million. With the income from it I could put a thirty-piece orchestra on the air an hour a week in a dozen key cities, playing the music of the future. I have some of it already written. If you think I'm touched, you're damn right I'm touched! So were Beethoven and Bizet touched, in their day. And the recordings. Dear God, the recordings I'll make! I mean I would make. Instead of reveling in that paradise, here I am. I spoke of millions. Would you like to hear the actual facts of my personal financial status?"

He turned and bent his head over the keyboard, and started two fingers of his right hand dancing over the black keys. He kept in one octave and touched so delicately that with my head cocked I could barely hear the faint discordant jangle. It set my teeth on edge, and I raised my voice. "I could lend you a buck."

He stopped. "Thanks. I'll let you know. Of course I eat here, so I won't starve. Would you care for a comment from Miss Marcy?"

He used both hands this time, and what came out was no jangle but a very pretty running coo. It was Miss Marcy to a T, with her variations and changes of pace, and he did it without any sign of a tune.

"Check," I said when he stopped. "I'd know her with my eyes shut. Beautiful."

"Thanks. Did Lewent tell you that I'm infatuated with Miss Riff?"

"No. Are you?"

"Oh, yes. If I played that for you, how I feel about Miss Riff, you'd be overcome, though I admit she isn't. That's why I wrote Lewent to come, because I was afraid she was going for my uncle, and I still am, I'm shivering with terror. And now, between you, you and he have bitched it up."

I told him that I disagreed and explained why. For one thing, I said, Lewent felt that getting the three suspects stirred up against him would not handicap him but help him. As soon as we found out which one it was he was going to start working on her, and he much preferred hostility to indifference as a base to start from. Thayer argued the point, but it was hard to hear him because he kept accompanying himself on the piano, and I requested him to move back to the bed, which he did. After more talk I decided I was wasting my time, since he couldn't furnish even a respectable guess on the question I was supposed to get answered, so I left him and moseyed back downstairs.

On the landing one flight down a maid in uniform with lipstick an inch thick gave me a sidewise glance, and I thought of wrangling her into the sewing room and pumping her, but decided to reserve it. On the floor below that I was tempted. Off to the right was the door to Lewent's room, and the big door straight ahead, which had been widened to admit the wheelchair, as Lewent had informed me, led to Huck's room. I could go and knock on it and, if I got a response, enter and ask him something. If there was no response, I could enter and take a look. A man who has been properly trained can do a lot of looking in five minutes, and it might be something quite simple, like a picture or a note in a drawer between shirts. But I reserved that too and descended another flight.

That was the floor Huck's study was on, but I couldn't use him at the moment, and there was no sight or sound of anyone, so I continued my downward journey and was on the ground floor. No one was in sight there either, but a sound came through where a door was standing half open, and I went and passed in. I have a habit of not making an uproar when I move. On a TV screen a man and woman were glaring at each other, with her breathing hard and him saying something. On a chair with her back to me sat Mrs. O'Shea, sipping a liquid from a glass and looking at the TV. I stepped across to a chair not far from her, sat, and focused on the screen. She knew I was there, certainly, but gave no sign. For some twenty minutes we sat and watched and listened to the story unfold. When it ended and the commercial started she went and turned it off.

"Good reception," I said appreciatively.

She eyed me. "You have your full share of gall, don't you? Did you want to see me?"

"I thought we might have a little private talk."

"Not now. I'll be busy in the kitchen for half an hour."

"Then later. By the way, Mr. Lewent invited me to stay for dinner, but under the circumstances I think I should ask you if it will be inconvenient."

"Mr. Lewent is Mr. Huck's guest, and if he invited you—of course. Mr. Huck eats in his room."

I told her yes, I knew that, and she left. In a moment I followed. Thinking it advisable to let Lewent know that he had invited me to stay for dinner, I went back up two flights of stairs and to his door, and knocked. No result. I knocked louder, and still no result. As I stood there the door of the elevator, ten paces down the hall, slid open, and out came the wheelchair. Huck, seeing me, stopped his vehicle and called, "You still here?"

"Yes, sir. If you don't mind."

"Why should I?"

He touched a button, and off it scooted, to the door of his room. He opened it and rolled through, and the door swung shut. I looked at my wristwatch, lifting it to close range in the dim light; it was two minutes past five. Thinking that Lewent might be taking a nap, I knocked again and, getting no response, I gave it up and went back to the stairs, descended, left the house, walked to Madison and down a block to a drugstore, went into a phone booth, and dialed a number.

Wolfe answered. I reported. "No progress. No nothing, except that if you get sick I've got a line on a nurse that can coo it out of you. I will not be home to dinner, God help me. I am calling to tell you that and to consult you."

"What about?"

"My brain. It must be leaking or I would never have let myself in for this."

He grunted and hung up. I dialed another number, got Lily Rowan, and told her I had decided I'd rather stay home and do crossword puzzles than keep my weekend date with her. She finally wormed it out of me that I was stuck on a case, if you could call it that, and said she would hold her breath until I rang her again.

Back at the house, admitted by the viqueen, I asked her where Miss Riff was. She didn't know. Miss Marcy? She didn't know. Mr. Lewent? She didn't know. I thanked her warmly and made for the stairs, wondering where the hell the client had got to. Probably sound asleep, and I resented it. On the third floor I knocked good and loud on his door, waited five seconds, turned the knob, and entered. I darned near walked on him. He was lying just inside, barely clear of the swing of the door, flat on his back, with one leg bent a little and the other one straight. I closed the door, squatted, unbuttoned his vest, and got a hand inside his shirt. Nothing. His head was at a queer angle. I slipped my fingertips under it, and at the base of the skull, or rather where there should have been a base, there was no resistance to pressure at all. The smashed edge of the skull was halfway up. But I couldn't feel any break in the skin, and there was no blood on my fingers.

I stood up and looked down at him, with my hands shoved in my pants pockets and my jaw set. After enough of that I stepped to where the little hall ended and the room proper began, and sent my eyes around slowly and thoroughly. Then I went and knelt by Lewent's head, with my knees spread, gripped his shoulders, and raised his torso till it was erect. There was nothing under him. I had a good look at the back of his head, then let him back down as before, got up and went and took his ankles and lifted his legs, and made sure there was nothing under that half of him. I moved to the door, held my ear to the crack for ten seconds, heard nothing, opened it and slipped through and pulled it shut, headed for the stairs, descended to the ground floor, and, no one appearing, let myself out.

At the drugstore on Madison Avenue I got dimes for a half-dollar before I went to the phone booth.

4

When Wolfe heard my voice on the phone he was peevish on principle, since I'm not supposed to disturb him when he is up in the plant rooms, and this was the second time in twenty minutes. I was peevish too, but not on principle.

"Hold it," I told him. "I am about to ask a favor. Twenty minutes ago I reported no progress, but I was wrong. We can't possibly disappoint our client, because he's dead. Murdered."

"Pfui."

"No phooey. I'm telling you—from a booth in a drugstore. I found the body, and I want to ask a favor."

"Mr. Lewent is dead?"

"Yes. In order to ask the favor I'll have to lead up to it—not a full report, but the high spots."

"Go ahead."

I did. I gave him no conversations verbatim, but described the cast of characters and the setting, and covered movements and events up to opening the door of Lewent's room. At that point I got particular.

"It would stand some questions," I told him. "The first ten feet inside the door it's not a room at all, merely a passage less than four feet wide. Beyond that is the room proper. The body is in that passage, diagonal, with the feet toward the door. When the door is opened wide its edge comes within ten inches of Lewent's right foot. There's a runner the length of the passage, an Oriental, not fastened down, and it's in place. The body's on it, of course. There is nothing disarranged in either the room or the passage. Everything is just as it was when I was there an hour earlier."

"Except Mr. Lewent." Wolfe's tone was dry and disgusted.

"Yeah. He was hit in the back of the head at the base of the skull with something heavy and hard enough to smash the whole bottom of the skull. The thing was comparatively smooth, because the skin is not broken, only bruised. No blood. I am not a laboratory, but on a bet there was only one blow and it came from beneath, traveling upward. The weapon is not in the passage—"

"Under him."

"No. I lifted him and put him back. Nor is it open to view in the room. Won't that stand some questions?"

"It will indeed. No doubt the police will ask them."

"I'm coming to that. I was not seen entering that room or leaving it. I might as well come on home, or, better still, go and keep my weekend date, if it weren't for one thing—the grand Lewent paid us. I've only been here three hours, and I doubt if I've been earning three hundred and and thirty-three dollars and thirty-three cents an hour, considering what's happened. Our client may not have been one of nature's top products, but to come here to do a job for him and just fiddle around while someone croaked him and then find his corpse is not my idea of a masterpiece. I don't like it. I won't like the remarks that will occur to Cramer and Stebbins if I phone the cops to say that Mr. Wolfe has had a client murdered while my back was turned and will they please come and take over. Nor will you."

"I won't hear them. Is there an alternative?"

"Yes. That's the favor I'm asking. My feelings are hurt."

"Naturally."

"I resent the assumption that it is perfectly okay to kill a client of yours practically in my presence. I want to ram that assumption down somebody's throat. I had already told Mrs. O'Shea that I am staying for dinner, and I ask your permission to do so. One of those people is stretched good and tight, waiting for the body to be found, and if I'm half as good as I think I am I'll see it or hear it or feel it. Anyhow I want to try."

"How sure are you that you're clear?"

"Completely. For a hair of my head on a rug, or a fingerprint, I was in there before. As for being seen, not a chance. I will mention that if you feel you owe Lewent some return for what he paid us, for which I could cite a couple of precedents, we're more likely to deliver this way than with the cops in command. And of course I can find the body any time I want to if that seems to be called for."

He grunted. "You won't be home to dinner."

I told him no and hung up, and sat a while, getting my mind arranged. The probability of the murderer's giving himself away while under the suspense of waiting for someone to find the body would be reduced by about nine-tenths if any word or look of mine aroused a suspicion that I already knew. Or would it? It might be better. Finally I left the booth, walked back to the house and rang the bell, and was admitted by the viqueen. She was as stolid as ever, so presumably there had been no discovery while I was out. As I started for the stairs down to the kitchen, intending to find Mrs. O'Shea, my name was called, and I turned to see Dorothy Riff coming through a door.

"I was looking for you," she said.

"I went out to phone Mr. Wolfe. What time do you go home?"

"I usually leave around six, but today . . ." She fluttered a hand. "I told Mr. Huck I'd stay until you're through." She glanced around. "This isn't very private, is it? Let's go in here."

She led the way into the room where I had watched the TV with Mrs. O'Shea, and through an arch into a larger room where a table toward one end was set with six places. She was telling me, "Since Mrs. Huck died we eat in here mostly, only I'm not often here for dinner. Sit down. We'll have cocktails later, upstairs with Mr. Huck."

We sat, not at the table. She was saying, "I was Mrs. Huck's secretary for four years, and when she died Mr. Huck kept me. He depends on me a lot. I wish you'd tell me something."

"Practically anything," I assured her. "Name it."

"Well—Mr. Huck feels sure that his brother-in-law is trying to blackmail him, and so do I. What do you think?"

Her gray-green eyes were at mine, intent, earnestly wanting to know what I thought. She couldn't possibly have been that free of guile, so I realized she was pretty good. "I'm afraid," I told her, "you'll have to fill in some. Usually a man knows whether he's being blackmailed or not without telling his good-looking secretary to ask a brainy detective what he thinks. Look out or you'll have your fingers in a hard knot and they won't come loose."

She jerked her fingers apart, extended a hand as if to touch me in appeal, and then took it back without reaching me.

"I wish we could talk just like two people," she said

hopefully. "I wish I knew how to ask you to help me."

"Nothing could be simpler. Help you what?"

"With Mr. Huck." Her eyes were holding mine. "I said he depends on me, and he always has, but now I don't know. Your coming here like this has made him suspicious. He knows that his nephew, Paul Thayer, is friendly with Mr. Lewent, and he thinks Paul and I are friends, and I think he suspects we are in a plot to blackmail him. He hasn't said so, but I think he does, and you know that isn't true. Why can't you tell me exactly how it stands, exactly what Mr. Lewent is after, and then possibly I can suggest something? I know Mr. Huck so well. I know how his mind works. Whatever it is you're after for Mr. Lewent, I'm sure you wouldn't want to make me lose a good job by getting Mr. Huck suspicious of me. Would you?"

"I should say not." I was emphatic. "But you said you agree with Huck, you feel sure that Lewent is trying to blackmail him. Since Lewent is our client, that hurts me, and I think we ought to clear it up. How about coming with me to ask Lewent and see what he has to say?"

"Now?"

"Right now."

She hesitated a moment, then stood up. "Come on."

In the hall we turned to the stairs instead of the elevator, and began the ascent. By the time we were up one flight, halfway, I had decided how to back out of it and postpone the discovery until I had had a chance to see a few more faces. But I didn't have to do any backing. When we reached the second landing and I turned to her, she had already stopped, and was standing, straight and stiff, her head tilted back a little for her eyes to slant up at me.

"No," she said.

"No what?"

"It wouldn't do any good. I can't! I can't talk with that man." A shiver ran over her. "He gives me the creeps! I don't want you—" She broke off, caught her lower lip with her teeth, and turned and headed along the hall toward the door to Huck's room. She didn't run, but she sure didn't loiter. When she reached the door she knocked, and, without waiting for an invitation, opened, entered, and shut the door. I moved noiselessly on the thick carpet, got to the wide door and put an ear to the crack, and heard a faint murmur of voices, much too low to catch any words. I stayed put, hoping for more decibels if they got agitated, and was still at the crack when a sound from above warned me. I was standing at the elevator door and had pressed the button by the time feet and shapely calves had come into sight on the stairs.

It was Sylvia Marcy. At the foot, instead of turning toward the next flight down, she turned my way and approached, with the intention, as I thought, of switching on the coo, but I was wrong. She did not merely toss me a glance, she kept her eyes straight at my face as she advanced, and even swiveled her head to prolong it until she was nearly even with me, but she kept right on going and uttered no sound. I could have stuck out a foot and tripped her as she passed. She went to the door to Huck's room, knocked, and entered without waiting. By then the elevator had stopped at my level, and I pulled the door open, stepped in, and pushed the button marked B.

Down in the basement I found the kitchen and walked in. It was big and clean and smelled good. An inmate I had not see before, a plump little woman with extra chins, was at a table peeling mushrooms, and Mrs. O'Shea was across from her, sorting slips of paper.

I spoke as I approached. "I should have told you, Mrs. O'Shea, I doubt if Mr. Lewent will show up for dinner. From what he said when he asked me to stay, I think he feels that under the circumstances it would be better if he were not there."

She went on with the slips a moment before she looked up to reply. "Very well. You were going to talk with me."

"I got sidetracked." I glanced at the cook. "Here?"

"As well here as anywhere."

I parked half of my fundament on the edge of the table. She resumed with the slips of paper, distributing them in piles, and as I watched her arm and hand in quick, deft movement I considered whether they could have struck the blow that killed Lewent, though my mind might easily have been better occupied, since actually a ten-year-old could have done it with the right weapon and the right frame of mind.

"From what you said earlier upstairs," I remarked, "I got the impression that you feel sorry for Mr. Lewent—in a way."

She compressed her lips. "Mr. Lewent is a thoroughly immoral man. And this trouble he's making—he deserves no sympathy from anyone."

"Then my impression was wrong?"

"I didn't say that." She sent the deep blue eyes straight at me, and they were much too cold to show sorrow for anyone or anything whatever. "Frankly, Mr. Goodwin, I am not interested in your impressions. I speak with you at all only because Mr. Huck asked us to."

"And I speak with you, Mrs. O'Shea, only because the man whose father built this house thinks he's been rooked and has hired me to find out. That doesn't interest you either?"

"No." She resumed with the slips of paper.

I eyed her. My trouble with her, as with the rest of them, was that it would take some well-chosen leading questions to jostle her loose, and all the best questions were out of bounds as long as Lewent was supposed to be still breathing.

"Look," I said, "suppose we try this. It's been more than two hours since I talked with you ladies up in the sewing room. Have you discussed the matter with Mr. Lewent? If so, when and where, and what was said?"

She sent me a sharp sidewise glance. "Ask him."

"I intend to, but I want—"

I got interrupted. A door in the kitchen's far wall was standing open, and through it, rolling almost silently on rubber tires, came a large cabinet of stainless steel. It was more than four feet high, its top reaching almost to the shoulders of Paul Thayer, who was behind it, pushing it. He rolled it across to the neighborhood of Mrs. O'Shea's chair and halted it.

"It's okay," he told her. "Just a bum wire, and I put in a new one. At your service. Invoice follows."

"Thank you, Paul." She had clipped the slips of paper together and was putting them in a drawer. "I'm glad you got it fixed. Mr. Goodwin is staying for dinner, so I suppose you'll bring him up for cocktails. Harriet, don't forget about the capers. Mr. Huck will not have it without the capers."

The plump little woman said she knew it, and Mrs. O'Shea left us, with, I noticed, the hip-swing in action, so it hadn't been a special demonstration for Huck.

I turned to Paul Thayer. "Lewent asked me to stay for dinner, but he's going to skip it, so do you think I rate a cocktail?"

"Sure, it's routine." He was matter-of-fact. "It was started by my aunt a couple of years ago when his legs went bad, and he has kept it up. How goes it? Have you spotted her?"

"Not to paste a label on." I aimed a thumb at the cabinet. "What's this, a dishwasher?"

"Hell no, a chow wagon. Designed by my aunt and made to order. Plug it in any outlet."

"It's quite a vehicle." I moved to it. "Mr. Wolfe ought to have one for breakfast in his room. May I take a look?"

"Sure, go ahead. I've got to wash my hands."

He went to the sink and turned on a faucet. I opened the door of the cabinet. There was room enough inside for breakfast for a family, with many grooves for the shelves so that the spaces could be arranged as desired. I slid a couple of them out and in, tapped the walls, and inspected the thermostat.

"Very neat," I said admiringly. "Just what I want for my ninetieth birthday."

"I'll remember and send you one." He was patting his hands with a paper towel.

"Do so." I neared him. "Tell me something. Did Lewent say anything—uh—disagreeable about Miss Riff to you this afternoon?"

He squinted at me. "What are you talking about?"

"I'm just asking. Did he?"

"No. I haven't seen Lewent this afternoon, not since he brought you up to my room and left us. Now I've answered, why did you ask?"

"Something someone said. Forget it."

"Who said what?"

I shook my head. "Later. If you don't want to forget it, I'll save it for after dinner. We'll be late for cocktails."

He tossed the paper towel at a wastebasket, missed it, growled something, went and picked it up and dropped it in, told me to come on, and led the way to the elevator.

The provision for drinks in Huck's room, which was large and lush with luxury, was ample and varied. They were on a portable bar near the center of the room, and alongside it was Huck in his wheelchair, freshly shaven, his hair brushed with care, wearing a lemon-colored shirt, a maroon bow tie, and a maroon jacket. Also the plaid woolen shawl that had covered his lower half had been replaced by a maroon quilted one. The room was lit softly but well enough, with lamps around—one of them a rosy silk globe at the end of a metal staff clamped to the frame of Huck's chair. As Thayer and I approached, Huck greeted us.

"Daiquiri as usual, Paul? And you, Mr. Goodwin?"

Having spotted a bottle of Mangan's Irish in the collection, I asked for that. Huck poured it himself, and Sylvia Marcy passed it to me. She had changed from her nurse's uniform to a neat little number, a dress of exactly the same color as Huck's shirt, as well as I could tell in that light; but she hadn't changed her coo. Mrs. O'Shea stood off to one side, sipping something on the rocks, and Dorothy Riff was there by the bar with a half-emptied long one. With my generous helping of Mangan's, I backed off a little and looked and listened. I have good eyes and ears, and they have had long training under the guidance of Nero Wolfe, but I couldn't see a movement or hear a word or tone that gave the faintest hint that one of them knew a body with a crushed skull was lying only fifty feet away, waiting to be found. They talked and got refills and laughed at a story Huck told. It was a nice little gathering, not hilarious, but absolutely wholesome.

At the end Huck made it more wholesome still. Mrs. O'Shea was starting to leave, and he called to her, and when she rejoined us he leaned over to reach a low rack at the side of his chair. Coming up with three little boxes bearing the name of Tiffany, he addressed the females.

"I'm sure you know, you three, that if it weren't for you my life would be miserable, crippled as I am. It is you who make it not merely bearable, but pleasant, really pleasant, and I've been thinking how I can show my appreciation."

He tapped the top box with a finger. "I was going to give these to you next Wednesday, my birthday, but I decided to do it today on account of Mr. Goodwin. His mission here, at the instance of my brother-in-law, is an imputation against you that I feel is utterly unjustified. Mr. Lewent is my wife's brother and so must be humored to the limit of tolerance; he was born in this house, and I will never challenge his right to live here and die here; but I want you to know that I have complete confidence in you, all three of you, and to make that as emphatic as possible I'm making this little presentation in the presence of Mr. Goodwin. Mrs. O'Shea?"

He extended a hand with one of the boxes, and the housekeeper stepped up and took it.

"Miss Riff?"

She took hers.

"Miss Marcy?"

She took hers.

As they got their eyes on their loot there were exclamations and expressions of delight. Sylvia Marcy let out a running broad coo that would have brought tears to my eyes if I hadn't been so busy using them.

"They're good timekeepers too," Huck, said, beaming.

Without being too vulgar I managed to get enough of a look to see that the presents were all wristwatches, apparently just alike, and if the red stones were Burma rubies Sylvia's coo was no exaggeration. Paul Thayer, looking flabbergasted, poured rum into his glass and gulped it down. Mrs. O'Shea, her little box clasped tightly in her hand, hustled from the room, and in a moment I heard the faint hum of the elevator. Before long I heard it again, and the wide door of the room opened and Mrs. O'Shea reappeared, pushing the stainless steel portable oven on rubber tires; it was nearly as tall as she was, and much bigger around. Miss Marcy moved the bar away, and Mrs. O'Shea put the oven there, beside Huck's chair.

"I'll just serve the soup?" she suggested.

"Now you know," Huck reproached her, "I'd rather do it myself." He swung a shelf of the chair around to make a table, and reached to a rack attached to the oven for a napkin.

There was a general movement toward the door, and I

joined it. In the hall Thayer and I were in the rear, and he muttered at me, "The damn old goat's got a caliph complex. All three of 'em!"

Going to the stairs to descend, we passed within a few feet of the door to Lewent's room. As far as I could tell, no one gave it a glance.

5

At ten minutes to eight, with the meal nearly over for the five of us at table, I said I didn't care for coffee, which wasn't true, excused myself on a pretext, and went up to the third floor, opened the door of Lewent's room, and entered.

I had decided to discover the body. They had all been agreeable enough at dinner, except Thayer, who was sulking about something, but it was plain that they were humoring me only because Huck had said his brother-in-law must be humored. No one said or did anything that gave me the slightest feeling of a hunch, and as dessert was being served and I took them in—Thayer scowling, and Mrs. O'Shea cold and cocky, and Dorothy Riff smirking at her new wristwatch, and Sylvia Marcy smiling at me like a sympathetic nurse—I had a strong feeling that it would be gratifying to arrange, for each of them, a prolonged interview with a cop, especially a good Homicide man. Also I had to admit that I had got nowhere with my idea of investigating a murder without disclosing that there had been one.

But now, in the narrow passage with the door closed, looking down at the corpse, I was doubling up my fists and setting my jaw. I would never have claimed that I was such a holy terror as a sleuth that no one had better risk a misdemeanor within a mile of me, but someone in this house had certainly had one hell of a nerve to perform on Wolfe's client like that with me wandering all over the premises. He looked pitiful there on the floor, and even smaller than when he was on his feet and breathing. I was more than willing for the performer to get tagged, the sooner the better, but not by a horde of city employees with me off in a corner being grilled by Lieutenant Rowcliff. On the other hand, at my rate of progress for the past two and a half hours, I would reach first base about a week from Tuesday.

I listened at the door a minute, opened it, passed through, and pulled it shut. I stood. There was no sight, sound, or smell of man or woman. I went to the stairs and started down quietly, which was no feat on the carpeted treads. At the bottom I stood again. Sounds of voices came up from the floor below, where dinner had been served, so they were still at the table. I headed down the hall for the door to Huck's study.

It was dark in there, but I closed the door before groping for the wall switch. It gave me light from ceiling fixtures, plenty, and I crossed to Huck's desk, which was actually two desks with an alley between them for his wheelchair, so that when he maneuvered into the alley he had desk space on both sides. There were three phones on the left, one a house phone and the other two labeled with their numbers, but the numbers were different. One of them was the number listed in the phone book, and I moved it forward, since it was the one I wanted to use, no matter how many extensions were on it. Needing two props, I looked around. One of them, exactly what I wanted, was on the other desk—a paperweight, a heavy ball of green marble with a segment sliced off to give it a base. For the other, there were hundreds of books available, and any of them would do. I would have liked to do some experimenting to find out how thick a book to use and how hard to hit it to get the effect I wanted, but under the circumstances it was not advisable. I got one about an inch thick, too intent on my program to notice the title, put it flat on the other desk, not the one the phone was on, lifted the receiver and dialed a number, and took the paperweight in my right hand.

Fritz answered, and I told him I was sorry to interrupt Wolfe's dinner if he wasn't finished, but I had to ask him something. After a wait his gruff voice came.

"Yes, Archie?"

I gave it pace and urgency. "I'm in Huck's study, and there may be someone on an extension, but I can't help it. If I call the cops now there'll be hell to pay, because— no, it's too long to explain. You absolutely refuse to leave the house on business, okay, but what about Saul? I need him. If you can get Saul—"

I cut myself off by bringing the paperweight down on the book and emitting the kind of sharp little agonized grunt a man may emit when he is solidly and accurately conked, and I let the receiver drop to the desk with a clatter. Also I collapsed onto the floor with enough racket to reach the transmitter, but not enough, I hoped, to alarm Huck up above or the quartet down below. Then I got back onto my feet and stood regarding the receiver lying on the table. That was a question I had left open. It might seem more natural for the cracker of my skull to replace the receiver, but if Wolfe dialed the number I certainly didn't want extensions ringing all over the place, and this way he would get a busy signal. So I let it lie.

It was now a matter of timing. Wolfe could conceivably try dialing the number, fail to get it, and shrug it off, but I doubted it. He was tough, but not that tough. He could phone the cops to please come and feel my pulse, but he never would, not after okaying my postponement of reporting a homicide. Then he would come himself, which was of course the idea, and I wanted to be at the door to let him in, but I did not want to leave the study at once, with the receiver out of its cradle. Two minutes would surely see him out of the house and on his way, but I would allow ten. I put the paperweight back, returned the book to its place on a shelf, and spent the rest of the time gazing at my watch. At the end of the tenth minute I replaced the receiver, left the room, and went down a flight to the entrance hall.

Dorothy Riff was there with her hat on, putting on her coat. If I had been thirty seconds later I would have been minus a member of the cast. She shot me a glance but offered no converse. I asked her courteously, "You're not leaving us?"

"Yes." She was brusque. "I'm going home. Any objection?"

"Yes." I was brusque too.

"Oh?" She cocked an eye. "You have?"

I nodded. "I've decided that you folks are too genteel for me. I'm the type that sticks thumbs in people's eyes, and this is the wrong setting for it. I have phoned Mr.

Wolfe to tell him that, and he agrees, and he's on his
way up here. He will particularly want to speak with you,
since it was you who suggested that his client is a black-
mailer, so if you don't mind waiting?"

She was frowning. "Nero Wolfe coming here?"

"Yes."

"What for?"

I waved a hand. "To detect."

"I don't believe it."

"Well, I won't try to sell you on it. Seeing is believing,
and seeing him you can believe anything. I have appointed
myself doorman, to let no one out, and to let him in."

"That's silly. I can go if I please."

"Sure you can. If you think Huck would like that."

She opened her mouth, shut it again, turned and made
for the stairs, and flew up. As she did so Paul Thayer
emerged from a door on the right, from the room where
the TV was, followed by Mrs. O'Shea and Sylvia Marcy.
They came on, Thayer demanding, "What's all the pow-
wow? Where's Miss Riff?"

I said I had told her that Wolfe was on his way to join
us, and she had gone up to tell Huck. The news did not
visibly impress Mrs. O'Shea, but Sylvia cooed something
appreciatively, and Thayer backed off, lowering his chin
and gazing at me from under his heavy brows. He had no
question or comment, but the two women did. Mrs.
O'Shea stated that she had always thought that professional
detectives caused more trouble than they cured, and now
she was sure of it. Miss Marcy said she would love to be
asked questions by Nero Wolfe, even if it wasn't something dreadful like murder, only her mind wasn't very
quick and she hoped he wouldn't get her tangled up about
some little thing.

A buzzer sounded, and I went and opened the door,
and Wolfe stepped in.

He gave me a piercing glance, swept his eyes around to
take in the others, returned to me, and muttered, "Well?"

"Miss Marcy," I said. "Mrs. O'Shea. Mr. Thayer. This
is Mr. Wolfe."

He inclined his head a quarter of an inch. "How do you
do." Again to me, louder and plainer, "Well?"

"There's an elevator," I told him, "which makes it

simple. We all take it. You and I get off on the next floor
and go to the study, and I explain the situation. The others
go to Mr. Huck's room on the floor above and tell him
we'll be up shortly, if that's how you would like to handle
it. If otherwise, you send me up with a message. Perfectly
simple. Your coat and hat?"

He let me take them. Putting them on a chair and making for the elevator, with them following, I heard Sylvia
cooing something at him but didn't catch it. One flight up
Wolfe and I got out, and I led the way down the hall to
the study, opened the door, and stood aside for him. When
I turned from closing the door he was facing me.

"Well?" he growled.

"Yes, sir. May I show you?"

I crossed to the desks and got between them. "I used
this phone." I touched it. "I put a book here." I tapped
the spot. "After dialing the number I took this in my right
hand." I picked up the paperweight. "At an appropriate
moment I hit the book with it, grunted, let the receiver
fall to the table, and dropped on the floor."

That was one of the two or three times, possibly four,
that I have seen him speechless. He didn't even glare. He
looked around, saw no chair that appealed to him, went
to a couch against a wall, sat, and buttressed himself by
spreading his arms and putting his palms flat on the couch.

"I forwent salad, cheese, and coffee," he said, "and came
at once."

"Yes, sir. I fully appreciate it. I can—"

"Shut up. You regard my rule not to leave my house
on a business errand as one of the stubborn poses of a
calculated eccentricity. It is no such luxury; it is merely
a necessity for a tolerable existence. Without such a rule
a private detective is the slave of all the exigencies of his
neighbors, and in New York there are ten million of them.
Are you too headstrong to understand me?"

"No. But I can—"

"Shut up." He had relaxed enough to tighten his lips
and glare. He shook his head. "No. Talk."

I moved a chair and planted it in front of him, knowing
that he disliked tilting his head to look up at people. When
I sat I was close enough to keep my voice down almost
to a whisper. "I'm fairly sure this room isn't wired for

sound," I said, "and that there's no one hiding in here, but we don't have to bellow. I would like to tell you what has happened in the last three hours. It will take seven minutes."

"I'm here," he growled. "Talk."

I did so, going overtime some, but not much. There was a pained and peevish look on his face throughout, but I could tell by his eyes that he was listening. Having covered the events, such as they were, I proceeded to cover me.

"When I left the dinner table and went upstairs," I declared, "I fully intended to glance in at the corpse and call the cops. But as I stood looking down at him I realized that I would have to call you first to tell you what I was going to do, and I didn't want to call you from here. I needed instructions. When the cops came, if I told them what Lewent had hired us to do, and the inmates here told them what I had said he had hired us to do, I would be in the middle of another of those goddam tangles that have been known to keep me on a straight-backed-chair in the DA's office for ten hours running. You would be in it too. I had to ask you to consider that and decide it, and I didn't want to leave here to go out to phone."

He grunted, not sympathetically.

"After all," I submitted, "no bones are broken, except Lewent's skull. You can tell me what to do and say, and go back home and have your salad and cheese and coffee. After you're safely outside I'll go up to our client's room to ask him something and will be horrified to find him dead, and will rush to notify the household and call the police. As for the thousand bucks he paid you, surely he would admit that you have earned it by coming up here to tell me how to manage things so that his death will cause us as little inconvenience as possible."

He eyed me. It was precisely the kind of situation that would normally have called for an outraged roar, in the privacy of his office, but here he had to hold it.

"Poppycock," he muttered bitterly. "You know quite well what you have done and are doing, and so do I. The police, and especially Mr. Cramer, would never believe that you would dare to trick me into coming here for anything less than murder, and they know that without a trick I wouldn't come at all. So I'll have to discuss murder with these people. Is there a decent chair in Mr. Huck's room?"

"Yeah, one that will do, but don't expect to like it."

"I won't." He stood up. "Very well. Let's go."

6

The chair problem in Huck's room required a little handling. After Wolfe had been introduced to Huck and Dorothy Riff, and Huck assented, without enthusiasm, to Wolfe's desire to discuss the affairs of his client Herman Lewent, there remained the fact that Paul Thayer was occupying the only chair that could take Wolfe without squeezing, and Thayer, who was still sulking, paid no attention to my polite hint. When I asked him to move and even said please, he gave me a dirty look as he complied.

As Wolfe sat and turned his head from left to right and back again, taking them in, and they focused on him, I was not utterly at ease because I had slid out from under the responsibility. He had said he would have to discuss murder with them, and in the heat of his resentment at my having foxed him into taking a two-mile taxi ride he might regard it as funny to manage it so that I would have not less to explain to the cops, but more.

Huck spoke. "I have explained to Mr. Goodwin that I tolerated his intrusion out of deference to my brother-in-law." His tone wasn't very deferential. "But now your barging in—frankly, Mr. Wolfe, there is a limit to my forbearance."

Wolfe nodded. "I don't blame you, sir. I return your candor and confess that the fault is Mr. Goodwin's. On account of a defect in his make-up he has botched his errand here so badly that I was compelled to intervene. When he phoned me, twice, some four hours ago, not from this house, I suspected that he had been so thoroughly bewitched by one of these women that his mental processes were in suspense. It hits him like that. When later he phoned again, this time from your study, my fear was verified, and I was even able to identify the witch."

He looked straight at Mrs. O'Shea, then at Miss Riff,

then at Miss Marcy, but got no return because they were all looking at me. I didn't mind, provided he was now willing to call it even.

He was going on. "Plainly there was no other alternative, so I came to supersede him; and now that I am here I refuse to employ the puerile stratagem that Mr. Lewent and Mr. Goodwin were determined to try. They should have known that their pretended concern about a large sum left secretly by Mr. Lewent's sister with one of you to be passed to him at her death—they should have known that none of you would take it seriously." He looked at Huck. "You, sir, even assumed that it was merely a black-mailing device, didn't you?"

"I thought it possible." Huck, being a millionaire, was giving no ground for a suit for slander. "You say it was a stratagem?"

"Yes." Wolfe flipped a hand. "Let's dismiss it. Slithering around looking for cracks is not to my taste. I'd much rather be forthright and tell you straight that I came here to discuss murder."

There were noises, but not explosive. Paul Thayer's head jerked up. My private reaction was absolutely unfavorable. Since he had blurted it out, a call to the police was in order right now, and exactly where would I be?

"Murder?" Huck was disbelieving his ears. "Did you say murder?"

"Yes, sir, I did." Wolfe was at a disadvantage. Working on an audience in his office, it wasn't difficult to keep all the faces in view, but there they made almost half a circle, with Huck in his wheelchair in the center, and Wolfe had to keep turning his head and moving his eyes. "There's no point," he declared, "in going on with the rigmarole started by Mr. Goodwin. I much prefer the directness and vigor of Mr. Lewent's original suggestion when he called at my office this morning to hire me. He suggested that Mr. Goodwin should come here and tell you that he, Lewent, suspected that one of these three women had murdered his sister, poisoned her, and that he had engaged me to investigate. I now propose—"

This time the noises could be called explosions, especially the one contributed by Mrs. O'Shea. Also she moved. She bounced out of her chair and started for the door, and when Wolfe sharply demanded where she was going and she didn't stop, I dived across and headed her off. White-faced, she ordered me, "Get out of my way! The dirty little rat!"

I held the pass. Wolfe's voice came. "If you're going for Mr. Lewent, madam, I beg you to consider. He came to me and paid me money because he lacked the spunk to tackle this himself. You can drag him in here, and the three of you can screech and scratch, but what good will it do? I'm willing to try to work this out, but not in pandemonium."

She turned and took a step.

"You should all realize," Wolfe told them, "what the situation is. You may think that this notion of Mr. Lewent's is preposterous, that he is in effect deranged, but that doesn't dispose of it or him. If he clings to it and speaks of it, it can become extremely ugly for all of you. Suing him for slander might settle him, but it wouldn't settle the stench. From the fact that he chose me to investigate for him, and from his paying me in advance what was for him a substantial sum, I assume that he has high regard for my sagacity, judgment, and integrity. If I am convinced that his suspicions are baseless and unmerited, I think I can persuade him to abandon them; and it may be that you can convince me here and now. Do you want to try?"

Paul Thayer threw his head back and haw-hawed. It didn't go over as well as it had when he and I were together in his room. They all looked at him, not admiringly, and when he subsided they transferred the looks to Theodore Huck. He was regarding Wolfe thoughtfully.

"I am wondering," he said, "if it would help for me to have a talk with my brother-in-law."

"No, it wouldn't," Sylvia Marcy said so positively that everyone glanced at her in surprise. Immediately she cooed. "I just mean," she cooed, "that he's a case. He is definitely a case."

Huck looked at Dorothy Riff. "What do you think?"

She didn't hesitate. The gray-green eyes were alert and determined. "I would like to know what it would take to convince Mr. Wolfe." She looked at him.

"That depends," Wolfe told her. "If, for instance, the source of the poison that killed Mrs. Huck has been satis-factorily established, and if none of you was connected with in in any way, I would be well on the road to conviction. According to Mr. Lewent, it was ptomaine, and all of you were on the premises at the time. Is that correct?"

"Yes."

"Good God," Paul Thayer protested, "you don't really mean it! You're actually going to ask us?"

"I'll ask you, Mr. Thayer, since you are not suspected by Mr. Lewent. Where did Mrs. Huck die? Here?"

Thayer looked at Huck. "What about it, Uncle Theodore? Do you want me to play?"

Huck nodded slowly. "I suppose so. Yes."

"Whatever you say." Thayer looked at Wolfe. "My aunt died in this house, in her bed, just about a year ago."

"Were you here?"

"Yes."

"Tell me about it. Just tell it, and I'll ask questions as required."

"Well." Thayer cleared his throat. "It was my uncle's birthday, and there was a little celebration here in this room. We were all here, we who are here now, and a few other people, four or five—old friends of my aunt and uncle. Do you want to know who they were?"

"Later, perhaps. Now just the event."

"We had drinks and things, and afterward a buffet dinner served in this room, plenty of wine—my aunt liked wine, and so does Uncle Theodore—finishing up with champagne, and some of us were fairly high, including me. In fact I finally got slightly objectionable, so my aunt said, and I left before the party broke up and went up to my room and made music. Did you ever play the piano while you were lit?"

Wolfe said no.

"Try it sometime. By the way, will you kindly tell me something? Why did one of these women poison my aunt? What for?"

"Speaking for Mr. Lewent, because she was on intimate terms with your uncle and wanted to marry him. Where there is room for a deed there is always room for a motive. That can—"

"You dare!" Mrs. O'Shea blazed. She was back in her chair.

"No, madam, I don't. I am only trying to learn if there is any cause for daring. Go on, Mr. Thayer?"

Thayer shrugged. "At some hour I quit making music and went to bed. In the morning I was told that my aunt had died, and the way it was described to me—it was quite horrible."

"Who described it?"

"Miss Marcy, and Mrs. O'Shea some."

Wolfe's eyes moved. "You saw it then, Miss Marcy?"

"Yes, I did." She was not cooing. "To say that one of us poisoned her, that's terrible."

"I agree. What did you see?"

"I was sleeping on the floor above this, and so was Mrs. Huck. She came and got me up; she was in great pain and didn't want to disturb her husband. I got her back to bed and called a doctor—it was after midnight—and I got Mrs. O'Shea, but there wasn't much we could do until the doctor came. It was a question about telling Mr. Huck—he couldn't even go in the room where she was, because the door was too narrow for his chair, but of course we had to tell him. She died about eight o'clock."

Wolfe went to Huck. "Naturally there was some inquiry —a death under those circumstances."

"Certainly." Huck was curt.

"Was there an autopsy?"

"Yes. It was ptomaine."

"Was the source identified?"

"Not by analysis." A spasm ran over Huck's face. He was having a little trouble with the controls. "Before dinner there had been a large assortment of hors d'oeuvres, and among them was a kind of pickled artichoke which my wife was very fond of. No one else had taken any of them, and apparently she had eaten them all, since there were none left. Since no one else was ill, it was assumed that the ptomaines, which were definitely present, had been in the artichokes."

Wolfe grunted. "I'm not a ptomaine scholar, but this afternoon I looked them up a little. Do you know how thoroughly the possibility of the presence of a true alkaloid was excluded?"

"No. I don't know what you mean."

"Isn't ptomaine an alkaloid?" Dorothy Riff asked.

"Yes," Wolfe conceded, "but cadaveric. However, for that there is the record. You were here the night of Mrs. Huck's death, Miss Riff?"

"I was here for the party. I left around eleven o'clock."

"Did you know that she was fond of pickled artichokes?"

"We all did. It was a kind of standing joke."

"How did you know that ptomaines are alkaloids?"

She flushed a little. "When Mrs. Huck died I read up about them."

"Why? Was there something about her death or about the artichokes that made you suspect something?"

"No! Of course not!"

Wolfe's head went right and left. "Did any of you suspect that Mrs. Huck's death was not accidental?"

He got a unanimous negative with no abstentions, but he insisted, "Have any of you felt, at any time, that the possibility of foul play was insufficiently explored?"

Unanimous again. Mrs. O'Shea snapped, "Why should we feel that if we didn't suspect anything?"

Wolfe nodded. "Why indeed?" He leaned back, cleared his throat, and looked judicious. "I am impressed, naturally, by the total absence of any currents of mistrust among you. Three women like you—young, smart, alive to opportunity, inevitably competitive in a household like this—are ideal soil for the seeds of suspicion if there are any around, but evidently none have sprouted in you. That is more than indicative, it is almost conclusive, and I could not expect, here in an hour or so, to reach the haven of certainty. It would be unreasonable to challenge you to convince me utterly; the law itself assumes innocence until guilt is demonstrated; and that leaves us only with the question, how much is it worth to you to have me employ my talent and energy to persuade Mr. Lewent that his suspicions are unfounded, and to keep him persuaded? Shall we say one hundred thousand dollars?"

They were unanimous again, this time with gasps. Miss Riff, quickest to find words, cried, "I told you it was blackmail!"

Wolfe showed them his palms. "If you please. I am indifferent to what you call it, blackmail or brigandage, but

it would be childish for you to suppose I would perform
so great a service for you as a benefaction. My spring of
philanthropy is not so torrential. The sum I named would
surely not be exorbitant. I'll be considerate on details; I
don't even insist on an IOU; it will be sufficient if Mr.
Huck will state, all of us hearing him, that he guarantees
payment of the full amount to me within one month. With
one provision, which I insist on, that no word of this arrangement ever reaches Mr. Lewent. On that I must have
explicit and firm assurance. I require the guarantee from
Mr. Huck because I know he is good for it and I know
nothing of the financial status of any of the rest of you,
and of course it is to his interest as well as yours that Mr.
Lewent should be persuaded that his suspicions are unfounded."

He took them in. "Well?"

"It's blackmail," Miss Riff said firmly.

Paul Thayer muttered, "Lewent picked a lulu when he
picked you."

Miss Marcy and Mrs. O'Shea were silent. They were
looking at Huck, obviously wanting a lead. Huck, his head
cocked to one side, was frowning at Wolfe, studying him,
as if in doubt whether he had heard correctly.

He spoke. "What makes you think," he asked, "that you
can manage my brother-in-law?"

"Mainly, sir, my self-conceit. I undertake it, and I too
am financially responsible. You guarantee to pay, and I
guarantee to deliver. You guarantee to pay me one hundred thousand dollars within one month, and I guarantee
that Mr. Lewent will not again accuse any person here
present of serious misconduct prior to this moment; and if
he does so I forfeit the entire amount paid me."

"Is there a time limit to your guarantee?"

"No."

"Then I accept it. I guarantee to pay you one hundred
thousand dollars within one month, as consideration for
the guarantee you have given, as stated by you. Is that
satisfactory?"

"Perfectly. Now the provision. It is understood by all of
you that no word of this arrangement is ever to get to Mr.
Lewent. You agree that you will give him no hint of it

either directly or indirectly. To indicate your agreement please raise your hands."

Mrs. O'Shea's hand went up first, then Miss Marcy's, then Miss Riff's. Wolfe asked, "Mr. Huck?"

"I thought it unnecessary. Certainly I agree."

"Mr. Thayer?"

With all eyes on him, Paul Thayer looked highly uncomfortable. He glanced at his uncle. "Oh, nuts," he said, and raised both hands as high as they would go.

"Then that's settled." Wolfe made a face. "Now I must go to work, and I must have your help. First I'll speak with Mr. Lewent privately, but it may be that after a preliminary I'll want to bring him in here for a brief colloquy. So you will please remain here a while—not long, I think." He got to his feet. "Archie, you said Mr. Lewent is in his room on this floor?"

I was a little tardy answering and moving because I was trying to see all their faces at once as they heard that we were going for Lewent. But Wolfe repeated my name, and I was up and with him, detouring around him to get to the door and open it. I led the way to Lewent's room, opened that door too, and, entering, flipped the wall switch for light and then stepped over Lewent's legs to get out of the way for Wolfe to come in. He did so and shut the door and stood looking down at his client.

"Lift him so I can see the back of his head."

That was no great strain, considering the size of the corpse and the fact that it was fairly stiff by then. When Wolfe finished his inspection and straightened up, I lowered it to the rug again, to its former position.

"As you know," Wolfe said, "it is regarded as undesirable to leave a corpse unguarded, especially when violence is indicated. I'll stay here. You will go and tell them what we have found, instructing them to remain together in Mr. Huck's room, and then call the police."

"Yes, sir. Call from Huck's rooms or go down to the study?"

"Either. As you choose."

"When the cops go into details with me, does my memory fail me anywhere besides my one trip to this room?"

"No. Everything else as it was."

"Including the way I got up here?"

"Yes. Confound it, go."

I went.

7

It had been twenty minutes to ten when Wolfe and I had left the gathering in Huck's room to go and have a talk with our client. It was a quarter past twelve, more than two and a half hours later, that we were in Huck's room again with a gathering—the same cast of characters with a few additions.

Meanwhile some two dozen highly trained city employees, including a deputy police commissioner and two assistant district attorneys, had put on an expert performance in the house that Herman Lewent's father had built and that Herman had after all managed to die in. I witnessed very little of the performance, since for most of the 155 minutes I was up in the sewing room answering questions and explaining previous answers, but I knew it was expert because I had seen most of them in action before. In one way at least it was too damn expert to suit me, because at a couple of points I wouldn't have minded a chance to exchange a few words with Wolfe, but I wasn't allowed to. We were expertly kept apart, and I had no sight or sound of him between nine-forty-five, when I left him guarding the corpse, and twelve-fifteen, when Sergeant Purley Stebbins, who has called me Archie eight times over the years in fits of absent-mindedness, came up to the sewing room for me and escorted me down to Huck's room.

It was the same cast of characters, but they were visibly the worse for wear. Huck himself, in his chair, still in the maroon tie and jacket, looked so pooped that I was surprised the official brass wasn't showing more consideration for a guy in his bracket whose bum legs gave them such a good excuse. It seemed likely that Paul Thayer had shown some temperament which required a little handling, since his tie was crooked and his hair mussed and a dick was standing at his elbow. On the whole the three women were apparently taking it a little better than the men, but they were by no means jaunty. Mrs. O'Shea sat stiff, her cold

blue eyes directed at Inspector Cramer, who was seated
near Wolfe. She didn't bother to glance at Purley and me
as we entered. And damned if Miss Riff and Miss Marcy
weren't holding hands! They were side by side on a couch,
sharing it with Assistant DA Mandelbaum and Deputy
Police Commissioner Boyle.

I had to hand it to Wolfe. He had the big chair he had
had before, and this time I hadn't been there to nab it for
him. And he didn't look fagged. As I came into range and
caught his eye, I thought, oh-oh, here we go. I knew that
look well. He was about to make some fur fly, or thought he
was.

He snapped at me, "Archie!"

"Yes, sir."

"Sit down. I have told Mr. Cramer I want to go home,
and as an inducement have offered some comments on
this affair, insisting on your presence. You have of course
answered all questions and given all the information you
have."

"Yes, sir."

"So have I. Move your chair—it obstructs my view of Mr.
Thayer. That's better. Mr. Cramer, I could have done this
much earlier—indeed, immediately after your arrival—but
you were not then ready to listen, and besides, there was
the possibility that your men would uncover something
that would weaken or even negate my assumptions. I don't
know that they haven't, so I need to ask a few questions."

Inspector Cramer's round red face was not sympathetic.
He rasped, "You didn't say you had questions, you said
you had comments. You practically said you know who
killed Lewent."

"I do, unless you know better. That's all my questions
are for. Are you ready to charge anyone?"

"No."

"Have you found a weapon that satisfies you?"

"No."

"Have you any evidence that would contradict an assumption that Lewent was killed elsewhere and his body
was transported to his room and dumped there?"

"No."

"Have you evidence pointing to any other place in this
house as the spot where he was killed?"

"No."

"Have you for any reason, evidential or speculative, excluded any of these people from suspicion?"

"No."

Boyle cut in from the couch. "How long do you intend to let this go on, Inspector?"

"You could have stopped it before it started," Wolfe said dryly. "But here's a comment. It is close to unbelievable that Lewent was killed where he was found. From such a blow he died instantly, and surely it was not struck in that narrow passage, particularly since it was moving upward at the moment of impact. With no sign of any struggle, with no displacement of the rug even, I can't believe that such a blow could be struck—"

"Skip it," Cramer growled. "Neither can we."

"You think he was killed elsewhere?"

"Yes."

"But you don't know where?"

"No."

Mandelbaum exploded, "What do you think this is, Wolfe, twenty questions?"

Wolfe ignored him. "My second comment. If he was killed elsewhere, why was the body moved? Because the murderer didn't want it found where it was. How was it moved? That's the real question. For vertical transport there was the elevator, but to and from the elevator, how? Was it dragged? That would leave marks, and of course you have looked for them. Have you found any?"

"No."

"Then it wasn't dragged. Carried? By whom? None of these women would be up to it. Lewent was undersized, but he weighed more than a hundred pounds. By Mr. Huck? It has been established that his legs will take him, with no burden, only a few steps. Then Mr. Thayer? He's all we have left, but why? That's another question I must ask you, Mr. Cramer. Why did Mr. Thayer kill Mr. Lewent?"

"I don't know."

"Have you even a decent surmise?"

"At present no."

"Neither have I. But there's another reason for excluding him, at least provisionally—that he's not a lunatic.

Only a lunatic would carry the body of a man he had just murdered up and down these halls at that time of day, with so great a probability of being seen. No, I think we may conclude that the body was neither dragged nor carried. It only remains—"

"By God!"

That was me. It popped out. It is not often that I let myself interrupt Wolfe when he has steam up and is rolling, but that time it hit me so hard that I didn't even know I was speaking. Eyes came to me, and Wolfe turned his head to inquire, "What is it, Archie?"

I shook my head. "I'll save it."

"No, we're through saving. What is it?"

"Nothing much, only that I suddenly realized that I actually saw the murderer in the act of transporting the corpse. I stood and looked straight at him while he was moving it, and we exchanged words. I don't like to brag, but don't you agree?"

"Yes, I think it likely—"

"This is one hell of a time to realize it," Sergeant Stebbins blurted at me.

"I suggest," Wolfe told him, "that you post yourself near Mr. Huck. He could have almost anything hidden around that chair, especially under that quilt, and I don't—"

"Just a minute, Wolfe." Mandelbaum had left the couch and was marching. "If you have any evidence against anyone, including Mr. Huck, we want to hear it or see it first."

"This is the man," Huck said in a voice not very steady, "who tried to extort one hundred thousand dollars from me!"

"And succeeded," Wolfe declared. "I'm by no means sure I couldn't collect, though—"

He stopped, startled. So was I, and the others. Purley Stebbins, who knew Wolfe from away back, had quietly moved to Huck's chair, at his right elbow, and all of a sudden Huck had jerked his head around and snarled at him in a spasm of fury, "Get away!" It was such a nasty snarl that Mandelbaum, also startled, forgot about Wolfe to stare at Huck. Purley, who had been snarled at by experts in his day, was unmoved.

"I offered comments, not evidence," Wolfe reminded them. "Here is one regarding the location and nature of the wound on Mr. Lewent's head, and the direction of the blow. Suppose I am Mr. Huck; here I am in my wheelchair, in my study. It is shortly before five in the afternoon, and my brother-in-law, Mr. Lewent, is with me. I have decided that he must die because I believe that he is a deadly menace to me. He has engaged Nero Wolfe, a detective who does not waste his time or talent on inanities, to start an investigation in my household on a pretext so absurd that it is manifestly a fake. I not only know that my wife would not have left a sum of money secretly to be given to her brother; I also know that he knows she would not have done that. In addition, Wolfe's assistant, Goodwin, in talking with my secretary and housekeeper and nurse, has dwelt on the possibility that one of them poisoned my wife, pretending that he is merely being facetious. One of them has told me about it. You might check that detail by inquiry."

"We have," Cramer admitted. "It was Miss Riff."

"Good. So I am convinced that my brother-in-law has become suspicious about his sister's death and therefore mortally threatens me. For the purpose of this comment, let us say the threat is possible disclosure of the fact that I poisoned his sister—my wife—by putting toxic material into a dish of artichokes. The inducement, which I realized, was inheritance of her wealth, amounting to millions. By the way, I don't suppose Mr. Huck can prove that Mr. Lewent did not come to his study between four and five o'clock?"

"No. He sent Miss Riff for him about half-past four. He says Lewent was with him about ten minutes and then left."

"Was Miss Riff present?"

"No. She left the house on an errand."

Wolfe nodded. "Good again. And in fairness to you, Mr. Cramer and gentlemen, it should be said that I have had one big advantage which you lacked. You haven't seen Mr. Huck propel himself in that vehicle, have you?"

They said no.

"I haven't either, but I have heard Mr. Goodwin describe the operation and was impressed. It was my memory of that description that put me on the path of these comments. At present Mr. Huck does not look as if he would care to demonstrate his machine, but you can manage that later. To go back: I am now Mr. Huck, here in my chair in my study, shortly before five o'clock." Wolfe pulled a handkerchief from his pocket and wadded it in his right hand. "This is a paperweight, a heavy ball of green marble with a segment sliced off. Actually it isn't in my hand, not quite yet; I merely have it ready, here on a shelf of my chair, holding down some papers. Archie, you are Mr. Lewent. Stand there in front of me, please—of course you could be either standing or sitting. A little closer would be more natural. Now I lift the paperweight with my right hand, and with my left pick up a paper to show you, but it slips from my fingers and falls to the floor. It's quite likely that before sending for you I practiced dropping that paper. Of course you bend over to retrieve it for me—that would be automatic, with me a cripple—and when you do so I strike with the paperweight."

I bent over, and he tapped me on the nape. I wasn't in the mood to ham it by dropping dead, but it didn't seem fitting to straighten up immediately, so I compromised by sinking to a knee.

"God save us," muttered Mrs. O'Shea, and there was no other sound. Wolfe went on. "In our relative positions, me sitting and you stooping, the impact would be upward on your skull. I must now move as fast as my disability will permit. Twenty seconds is enough to satisfy me that no second blow is needed; you are dead. I am sound and strong from the hips up, and in another twenty seconds I have you lifted and draped over my legs and covered with the shawl that I am never without. I push a button and grasp the lever, and off we go. I must dump you on another floor. It is a risk, certainly, but I must take it."

"Evidence, damn it," Mandelbaum growled.

"By all means," Wolfe conceded, "and the sooner the better. You might start by learning if the paperweight fits the dent in the skull; I think you'll find that it does. Examine the plaid shawl that was used for a shroud; you may find hairs of Lewent's head. You had already concluded that the murder was not committed in Lewent's room; I challenge you to explain how the body was transported if not on Mr. Huck's chair. I confess it is a pity that the day was dying and the light in the hall was dim when

Mr. Goodwin stood at the door of Lewent's room and saw Mr. Huck, in his chair, emerge from the elevator and head for his room. Mr. Goodwin has sharp eyes, and in better light he would probably have noticed that the hump under the shawl was larger than it should have been. Of course his presence forced Mr. Huck to retreat to his own room with his cargo temporarily, but Mr. Goodwin left almost at once —left the house to phone me—and Mr. Huck finished the transport. That must have been the hardest part for him, since the door to Lewent's room was too narrow for his chair."

Wolfe tilted his head to Mandelbaum, who was still standing. "But I like this for evidence. To me, in fact, this alone is absolutely conclusive. You have questioned all of us at length, and you know what was said in this room immediately prior to the discovery of the body. You know that in the presence of five witnesses I extorted from Mr. Huck a promise to pay me a large sum of money—for what? For my reciprocal promise that Mr. Lewent would not again pester any of them with accusations! It is inconceivable that Mr. Huck could be such an ass as to agree to any such bargain if he had thought Lewent was still alive. Word of it, from Mr. Thayer if no one else, was sure to reach Lewent, and he, thinking I had betrayed him by taking a bribe from the enemy, would have had his suspicions redoubled instead of stilled."

Wolfe shook his head. "No. Unquestionably Huck knew then that Lewent was dead; that certainty struck me the moment I saw the corpse. Not only that; by agreeing to my preposterous proposal Huck was confessing to his guilt. He thought I was blackmailing him, and, momentarily at least, he thought he had to submit. I had tackled him before witnesses, and he would have to get me alone to find out how much I knew and how I might be dealt with. But for the terror of his guilt, he would have scorned me as a witling; when I made my proposal and demand, he would have sent for his brother-in-law and denounced me to him. Instead—but you know what he did, and look at him now."

Most of those present did look at him, but three did not, and it went to show how men's minds work. The three were Assistant District Attorney Mandelbaum, Deputy Police

Commissioner Boyle, and Inspector Cramer. They, three high-ranking officers of the law, were gazing resentfully and indignantly, not at the murderer who had just been exposed, but at the man who had exposed him. Not that you could blame them much. They would have to charge Huck and take him, that was clear, but they were by no means ready for a judge and jury; and Huck had enough dough to hire the ten best lawyers in town.

Cramer rose to his feet, shot a glance to his right to make sure Sergeant Stebbins was standing by, and moved to plant himself in front of Wolfe.

"Yeah, look at him now," he growled, "and look at you! You and your helpful comments! That bargain you offered him—you say it's inconceivable that he could have been such an ass as to agree to it if he had thought Lewent was still alive. Okay, but what about you? It's also inconceivable that you could have been such an ass as to offer it if you had thought Lewent was still alive. God knows I could call you plenty of things, but not an ass. That stunt Goodwin pulled to get you up here—don't try to tell me he would have pulled it, or that you would have come, if you hadn't both known Lewent had been murdered! I want a comment on that!"

"Pfui," Wolfe said mildly. "Don't you think you have enough on your hands without—"

He stopped to watch a performance, and this time it went to show how women's minds work. Mrs. O'Shea was on her feet and moving, slowly as if in a trance, toward her employer, with tears streaming from her eyes and down her cheeks and her arms crossed on her chest. She stopped three steps short of him.

"This is from heaven," she said, in so low a voice that she could barely be heard. "The terror in my heart—oh, God, so long! You lied to me, and somewhere in me I knew it all the time! She did find out about us—she found out and told you so, and you killed her. Thank heaven, oh, thank heaven—"

Inspector Cramer was there and had her elbow. Another woman's mind was working too. Sylvia Marcy left the couch, walked across through the group to the wheelchair, and placed an object on Theodore Huck's lap, on top of the maroon quilt. It was after she had moved away and started for the door that I saw what the object was—a wristwatch with a ring of red stones, maybe rubies.

I can't report on the fate of the other two gifts whose presentation had been precipitated by my presence. Months have passed, and only last week a jury convicted Theodore Huck of first-degree murder, but as far as I know Mrs. O'Shea and Miss Riff still have their watches.

The Zero Clue

1

It began with a combination of circumstances, but what doesn't? To mention just one, if there hadn't been a couple of checks to deposit that morning I might not have been in that neighborhood at all.

But I was, and, approving of the bright sun and the sharp clear air as I turned east off Lexington Avenue into Thirty-seventh Street, I walked some forty paces to the number and found it was a five-story yellow brick, clean and neat, with greenery in tubs flanking the entrance. I went in. The lobby, not much bigger than my bedroom, had a fancy rug, a fireplace without a fire, more greenery, and a watchdog in uniform who challenged me with a suspicious look.

As I opened my mouth to meet his challenge, circumstances combined. A big guy in a dark blue topcoat and homburg, entering from the street, breezed past me, heading for the elevator, and as he did so the elevator door opened and a girl emerged. Four of us in that undersized lobby made a crowd, and we had to maneuver. Meanwhile I was speaking to the watchdog.

"My name's Goodwin, and I'm calling on Leo Heller."

Gazing at me, his expression changing, he blurted at me, "Ain't you Archie Goodwin works for Nero Wolfe?"

The girl, making for the exit, stopped a step short of it and turned, and the big guy, inside the elevator, blocked the door from closing and stuck his head out, while the watchdog was going on, "I've saw your picture in the paper, and look, I want Nero Wolfe's autograph."

It would have been more to the point if he had wanted mine, but I'm no hog. The man in the elevator, which was self-service, was letting the door close, but the girl was standing by, and I hated to disappoint her by denying I was me, as of course I would have had to do if I had been there on an operation that needed cover.

I'll have to let her stand there a minute while I explain that I was actually not on an operation at all. Chiefly, I was satisfying my curiosity. At five in the afternoon the day before, in Nero Wolfe's office, there had been a phone call. After taking it I had gone to the kitchen—where Fritz was boning a pig's head for what he calls *fromage de cochon*—to get a glass of water, and told Fritz I was going upstairs to do a little yapping.

"He is so happy up there," Fritz protested, but there was a gleam in his eye. He knows darned well that if I quit yapping the day would come when there would be no money in the bank to meet the payroll, including him.

I went up three flights, on past the bedroom floors to the roof, where ten thousand square feet of glass in aluminum frames make a home for ten thousand orchid plants. The riot of color on the benches of the three rooms doesn't take my breath any more, but it is unquestionably a show, and as I went through that day I kept my eyes straight ahead to preserve my mood for yapping intact. However, it was wasted. In the intermediate room Wolfe stood massively, with an Odontoglossum seedling in his hand, glaring at it, a mountain of cold fury, with Theodore Horstmann, the orchid nurse, standing nearby with his lips tightened to a thin line.

As I approached, Wolfe transferred the glare to me and barked savagely, "Thrips!"

I did some fast mood shifting. There's a time to yap and a time not to yap. But I went on.

"What do you want?" he rasped.

"I realize," I said politely but firmly, "that this is ill timed, but I told Mr. Heller I would speak to you. He phoned—"

"Speak to me later! If at all!"

"I'm to call him back. It's Leo Heller, the probability

wizard. He says that calculations have led him to suspect
that a client of his may have committed a serious crime, but
it's only a suspicion and he doesn't want to tell the police
until it has been investigated, and he wants us to investigate. I asked for details, but he wouldn't give them on the
phone. I thought I might as well run over there now—it's
over on East Thirty-seventh Street—and find out if it looks
like a job. He wouldn't—"

"No!"

"My eardrums are not insured. No what?"

"Get out!" He shook the thrips-infested seedling at me.
"I don't want it! That man couldn't hire me for any conceivable job on any imaginable terms! Get out!"

I turned, prompt but dignified, and went. If he had
thrown the seedling at me I would of course have dodged,
and the fairly heavy pot would have sailed on by and
crashed into a cluster of Calanthes in full bloom, and God
only knew what Wolfe would have done then.

On my way back down to the office I was wearing a grin.
Even without the thrips, Wolfe's reaction to my message
would have been substantially the same, which was why
I had been prepared to yap. The thrips had merely keyed
it up. Leo Heller had been tagged by fame, with articles
about him in magazines and Sunday newspapers. While
making a living as a professor of mathematics at Underhill
College, he had begun, for amusement, to apply the laws of
probability, through highly complicated mathematical formulas, to various current events, ranging from ball games
and horse races to farm crops and elections. Checking back
on his records after a couple of years, he had been startled
and pleased to find that the answers he had got from his
formulas had been 86.3 per cent correct, and he had written a piece about it for a magazine. Naturally requests had
started coming from all kinds of people for all kinds of
calculations, and he had granted some of them to be oblig-
ing, but when he had tried telling a woman in Yonkers
where to look for thirty-one thousand dollars in currency
she had lost, and she had followed instructions and found
it and had insisted on giving him two grand, he sidestepped to a fresh slant on the laws of probability as
applied to human problems and resigned his professorship.

That had been three years ago, and now he was sitting

pretty. It was said that his annual take was in six figures, that he returned all his mail unanswered, accepting only clients who called in person, and that there was nothing on earth he wouldn't try to dope a formula for, provided he was furnished with enough factors to make it feasible. It had been suggested that he should be hauled in for fortunetelling, but the cops and the DA's office let it lay, as well they might, since he had a college degree and there were at least a thousand fortunetellers operating in New York who had never made it through high school.

It wasn't known whether Heller was keeping his percentage up to 86.3, but I happened to know it wasn't goose eggs. Some months earlier a president of a big corporation had hired Wolfe to find out which member of his staff was giving trade secrets to a competitor. I had been busy on another case at the time, and Wolfe had put Orrie Cather on the collection of details. Orrie had made a long job of it, and the first we knew we were told by the corporation president that he had got impatient and gone to Leo Heller with the problem, and Heller had cooked up a formula and come out with an answer, the name of one of the junior vice-presidents, and the junior VP had confessed! Our client freely admitted that most of the facts he had given Heller for the ingredients of his formula had been supplied by us, gathered by Orrie Cather, and he offered no objection to paying our bill, but Wolfe was so sore he actually told me to send no bill—an instruction I disregarded, knowing how he would regret it after he had cooled off. However, as I was aware through occasional mutterings from him, he still had it in for Leo Heller, and taking on any kind of job for him would have been absolutely off the program that day or any other day, even if there had been no thrips within a mile of Thirty-fifth Street.

Back downstairs in the office, I phoned Heller and told him nothing doing. "He's extremely sensitive," I explained, "and this is an insult. As you know, he's the greatest detective that ever lived, and—do you know that?"

"I'm willing to postulate it," Heller conceded in a thin voice that tended to squeak. "Why an insult?"

"Because you want to hire Nero Wolfe—meaning me, really—to collect facts on which you can base a decision whether your suspicion about your client is justified. You might as well try to hire Stan Musial as bat boy. Mr. Wolfe doesn't sell the raw material for answers; he sells answers."

"I'm quite willing to pay him for an answer, any amount short of exorbitance, and in cash. I'm gravely concerned about this client, this situation, and my data is insufficient. I shall be delighted if with the data I get an answer from Mr. Wolfe, and—"

"And," I put in, "if his answer is that your client has committed a serious crime, as you suspect, he decides whether and when to call a cop, not you. Yes?"

"Certainly." Heller was eager to oblige. "I do not intend or desire to shield a criminal—on the contrary."

"Okay. Then it's like this. It wouldn't do any good for me to take it up with Mr. Wolfe again today because his feelings have been hurt. But tomorrow morning I have to go to our bank on Lexington Avenue not far from your place, to deposit a couple of checks, and I could drop in to see you and get the sketch. I suspect that I make this offer mostly because I'm curious to see what you look like and talk like, but I haven't enough data to apply the laws of probability to it. Frankly, I doubt if Mr. Wolfe will take this on, but we can always use money, and I'll try to sell him. Shall I come?"

"What time?"

"Say a quarter past ten."

"Come ahead. My business day begins at eleven. Take the elevator to the fifth floor. An arrow points right, to the waiting room, but go left to the door at the end of the hall, and push the button, and I'll let you in. If you're on time we'll have more than half an hour."

"I'm always on time."

That morning I was a little early. It was nine minutes past ten when I entered the lobby on Thirty-seventh Street and gave the watchdog my name.

2

I told the watchdog I would try to get Nero Wolfe's autograph for him, and wrote his name in my notebook: Nils Lamm. Meanwhile the girl stood there facing us, frowning

at us. She was twenty-three or -four, up to my chin, and
without the deep frown her face would probably have deserved attention. Since she showed no trace of embarrassment, staring fixedly at a stranger, I saw no reason why I
should, but something had to be said, so I asked her, "Do
you want one?"

She cocked her head. "One what?"

"Autograph. Either Mr. Wolfe's or mine, take your
pick."

"Oh. You are Archie Goodwin, aren't you? I've seen
your picture too."

"Then I'm it."

"I—" She hesitated, then made up her mind. "I want to
ask you something."

"Shoot."

Someone trotted in from the street, a brisk female in
mink, executive type, between twenty and sixty, and the
girl and I moved aside to clear the lane to the elevator. The
newcomer told Nils Lamm she was seeing Leo Heller and
refused to give her name, but when Lamm insisted she
coughed it up: Agatha Abbey, she said, and he let her take
the elevator. The girl told me she had been working all
night and was tired, and we went to a bench by the fireplace. Close up, I would still have said twenty-three or
-four, but someone or something had certainly been harass-
ing her. Naturally there was a question in my mind about
the night work.

She answered it. "My name's Susan Maturo, and I'm a
registered nurse."

"Thanks. You know mine, and I'm a registered detective."

She nodded. "That's why I want to ask you something. If
I hired Nero Wolfe to investigate a—a matter, how much
would it cost?"

I raised my shoulders half an inch and let them down.
"It all depends. The kind of matter, the amount of time
taken, the wear and tear on his brain, the state of your
finances. . . ."

I paused, letting it hang, to return a rude stare that was
being aimed at us by another arrival, a thin tall bony specimen in a brown suit that badly needed pressing, with a
bulging briefcase under his arm. When my gaze met his he

called it off and turned and strode to the elevator, without any exchange with Nils Lamm.

I resumed to Susan Maturo. "Have you got a matter, or are you just researching?"

"Oh, I've got a matter." She set her teeth on her lip—nice teeth, and not a bad lip—and kept them that way a while, regarding me. Then she went on, "It hit me hard, and it's been getting worse in me instead of better. I began to be afraid I was going batty, and I decided to come to this Leo Heller and see what he could do, so I came this morning, but I was sitting up there in his waiting room—two people were already there, a man and a woman—and it went all through me that I was just being bitter and vindictive, and I don't think I'm really like that—I'm pretty sure I never have been—"

Apparently she needed some cooperation, so I assured her, "You don't look vindictive."

She touched my sleeve with her fingertips to thank me. "So I got up and left, and then as I was leaving the elevator I heard that man saying your name and who you are, and it popped into my head to ask you. I asked how much it would cost to have Nero Wolfe investigate, but that was premature, because what I really want is to tell him about it and get his advice about investigating."

She was dead serious and she was all worked up, so I arranged my face and voice to fit. "It's like this," I told her, "for that kind of approach to Mr. Wolfe, with no big fee in prospect, some expert preparation is required, and I'm the only expert in the field." I glanced at my wrist and saw 10:19. "I've got a date, but I can spare five minutes if you want to brief me on the essentials, and then I'll tell you how it strikes me. What was it that hit you?"

She looked at me, shot a glance at Nils Lamm, who couldn't have moved out of earshot in that lobby if he had wanted to, and came back to me. Her jaw quivered, and she clamped it tight and held it for a moment, then released it and spoke. "When I start to talk about it, it sticks in my throat and chokes me, and five minutes wouldn't be enough, and anyway I need someone old and wise like Nero Wolfe. Won't you let me see him?"

I promised to try. I told her that it would be hard to find any man in the metropolitan area more willing to help an

attractive girl in distress than I was, but it would be a
waste of time and effort for me to take her in to Wolfe
cold, and though I was neither old nor wise she would
have to give me at least a full outline before I could furnish
either an opinion or help. She agreed that that was reasonable and gave me her address and phone number, and we
arranged to communicate later in the day. I went and
opened the door for her, and she departed.

On the way up in the elevator my watch said 10:28, so I
wasn't on time after all, but we would still have half an
hour before Heller's business day began. On the fifth floor
a plaque on the wall facing the elevator was lettered LEO
HELLER, WAITING ROOM, with an arrow pointing right, and
at that end of the narrow hall a door bore the invitation,
WALK IN. I turned left, toward the other end, where I
pushed a button beside a door, noticing as I did so that
the door was ajar a scanty inch. When my ring brought no
response, and a second one, more prolonged, didn't either,
I shoved the door open, crossed the sill, and called Heller's
name. No reply. There was no one in sight.

Thinking that he had probably stepped into the waiting
room and would soon return, I glanced around to see what
the lair of a probability wizard looked like, and was impressed by some outstanding features. The door, of metal,
was a good three inches thick, either for security or for
soundproofing, or maybe both. If there were any windows
they were behind the heavy draperies; the artificial light
came indirectly from channels in the walls just beneath
the ceiling. The air was conditioned. There were locks on
all the units of a vast assembly of filing cabinets that took
up all the rear wall. The floor, with no rugs, was tiled with
some velvety material on which a footfall was barely audible.

The thick door was for soundproofing. I had closed it,
nearly, on entering, and the silence was complete. Not a
sound of the city could be heard, though the clang and
clatter of Lexington Avenue was nearby one way and
Third Avenue the other.

I crossed for a look at the desk, but there was nothing
remarkable about it except that it was twice the usual size.
Among other items it held a rack of books with titles that
were not tempting, an abacus of ivory or a good imitation,

and a stack of legal-size working pads. Stray sheets of paper were scattered, and a single pad had on its top sheet some scribbled formulas that looked like doodles by Einstein. Also a jar of sharpened lead pencils had been overturned, and some of them were in a sort of a pattern near the edge of the desk.

I had been in there ten minutes, and no Heller; and when, at eleven o'clock by schedule, Wolfe came down to the office from his morning session with the orchids, it was desirable that I should be present. So I went, leaving the door ajar as I had found it, walked down the hall to the door of the waiting room at the other end, and entered.

This room was neither air-conditioned nor sound-proofed. Someone had opened a window a couple of inches, and the din was jangling in. Five people were here and there on chairs; three of them I had seen before: the big guy in the dark blue topcoat and homburg, the brisk female in mink who called herself Agatha Abbey, and the tall thin specimen with a briefcase. Neither of the other two was Leo Heller. One was a swarthy little article, slick and sly, with his hair pasted to his scalp, and the other was a big blob of an overfed matron with a spare chin.

I addressed the gathering. "Has Mr. Heller been in here?"

A couple of them shook their heads, and the swarthy article said hoarsely, "Not visible till eleven o'clock, and you take your turn."

I thanked him, left, and went back to the other room. Still no Heller. I didn't bother to call his name again, since even if it had flushed him I would have had to leave immediately. So I departed. Down in the lobby I again told Nils Lamm I'd see what I could do about an autograph. Outside, deciding there wasn't time to walk it, I flagged a taxi. Home again, I hadn't been in the office more than twenty seconds when the sound came of Wolfe's elevator descending.

That was a funny thing. I'm strong on hunches, and I've had some beauts during the years I've been with Wolfe, but that day there wasn't the slightest glimmer of something impending. You might think that was an ideal spot for a hunch, but no, not a sign of a tickle. I was absolutely blithe as I asked Wolfe how the anti-thrips campaign was doing, and later, after lunch, as I dialed the number Susan Maturo had given me, though I admit I was a little dampened when I got no answer, since I had the idea of finding out someday how she would look with the frown gone.

But still later, shortly after six o'clock, I went to answer the doorbell and through the one-way glass panel saw Inspector Cramer of Manhattan Homicide there on the stoop. There was an instant reaction in the lower third of my spine, but I claim no credit for a hunch, since after all a homicide inspector does not go around ringing doorbells to sell tickets to the Policemen's Annual Ball.

I let him in and took him to the office, where Wolfe was drinking beer and scowling at three United States senators on television.

3

Cramer, bulky and burly, with a big red face and sharp and skeptical gray eyes, sat in the red leather chair near the end of Wolfe's desk. He had declined an offer of beer, the TV had been turned off, and the lights had been turned on.

Cramer spoke. "I dropped in on my way down, and I haven't got long." He was gruff, which was normal. "I'd appreciate some quick information. What are you doing for Leo Heller?"

"Nothing." Wolfe was brusque, which was also normal.

"You're not working for him?"

"No."

"Then why did Goodwin go to see him this morning?"

"He didn't."

"Hold it," I put in. "I went on my own, just exploring. Mr. Wolfe didn't know I was going, and this is the first he's heard of it."

There were two simultaneous looks of exasperation—Cramer's at Wolfe, and Wolfe's at me. Cramer backed his up with words. "For God's sake. This is the rawest one you ever tried to pull! Been rehearsing it all afternoon?"

Wolfe let me go temporarily, to cope with Cramer. "Pfui. Suppose we have. Justify your marching into my house to demand an accounting of Mr. Goodwin's movements. What if he did call on Mr. Heller? Has Mr. Heller been found dead?"

"Yes."

"Indeed." Wolfe's brows went up a little. "Violence?"

"Murdered. Shot through the heart."

"On his premises?"

"Yeah. I'd like to hear from Goodwin."

Wolfe's eyes darted to me. "Did you kill Mr. Heller, Archie?"

"No, sir."

"Then oblige Mr. Cramer, please. He's in a hurry."

I obliged. First telling about the phone call the day before, and Wolfe's refusal to take on anything for Heller, and my calling Heller back, I then reported on my morning visit at Thirty-seventh Street, supplying all details, except that I soft-pedaled Susan Maturo's state of harassment, putting it merely that she asked me to arrange for her to see Wolfe and didn't tell me what about. When I had finished, Cramer had a few questions. Among them:

"So you didn't see Heller at all?"

"Nope."

He grunted. "I know only too well how nosy you are, Goodwin. There were three doors in the walls of that room besides the one you entered by. You didn't open any of them?"

"Nope."

"One of them is the door to the closet in which Heller's body was found by a caller, a friend, at three o'clock this afternoon. The medical examiner says that the sausage and griddle cakes he ate for breakfast at nine-thirty hadn't been in him more than an hour when he died, so it's practically certain that the body was in the closet while you were there in the room. As nosy as you are, you're telling me that you didn't open the door and see the body?"

"Yep. I apologize. Next time I'll open every damn door in sight."

"A gun had been fired. You didn't smell it?"

"No. Air-conditioned."

"You didn't look through the desk drawers?"

"No. I apologize again."

"We did." Cramer took something from his breast pocket. "In one drawer we found this envelope, sealed.

On it was written in pencil, in Heller's hand, 'Mr. Nero Wolfe.' In it were five one-hundred-dollar bills."

"I'm sorry I missed that," I said with feeling.

Wolfe stirred. "I assume that has been examined for fingerprints."

"Certainly."

"May I see it, please?"

Wolfe extended a hand. Cramer hesitated a moment, then tossed it across to the desk, and Wolfe picked it up. He took out the bills, crisp new ones, counted them, and looked inside.

"This was sealed," he observed dryly, "with my name on it, and you opened it."

"We sure did." Cramer came forward in his chair with a hand stretched. "Let me have it."

It was a demand, not a request, and Wolfe reacted impulsively. If he had taken a second to think he would have realized that if he claimed it he would have to earn it, or at least pretend to, but Cramer's tone of voice was the kind of provocation he would not take. He returned the bills to the envelope and put it in his pocket.

"It's mine," he stated.

"It's evidence," Cramer growled, "and I want it."

Wolfe shook his head. "Evidence of what? As an officer of the law, you should be acquainted with it " He tapped his pocket with a fingertip. "My property. Connect it or connect me, with a crime."

Cramer was controlling himself, which wasn't easy under the circumstances. "I might have known," he said bitterly. "You want to be connected with a crime? Okay. I don't know how many times I've sat in this chair and listened to you making assumptions. I'm not saying you never make good on them, I just say you're strong on assumptions. Now I've got some of my own to offer, but first here are a few facts. In that building on Thirty-seventh Street, Heller lived on the fourth floor and worked on the fifth, the top floor. At five minutes to ten this morning, on good evidence, he left his living quarters to go up to his office. Goodwin says he entered that office at ten-twenty-eight, so if the body was in the closet when Goodwin was there—and it almost certainly was—Heller was killed between nine-fifty-five and ten-twenty-eight. We can't find anyone who heard the shot, and the way that room is proofed we probably never will. We've tested it."

Cramer squeezed his eyes shut and opened them again, a trick of his. "Very well. From the doorman we've got a list of everyone who entered the place during that period, and most of them have been collected, and we're getting the others. There were six of them. The nurse, Susan Maturo, left before Goodwin went up, and the other five left later, at intervals, when they got tired waiting for Heller to show up—according to them. As it stands now, and I don't see what could change it, one of them killed Heller. Any of them, on leaving the elevator at the fifth floor, could have gone to Heller's office and shot him, and then to the waiting room."

Wolfe muttered, "Putting the body in the closet?"

"Of course, to postpone its discovery. If someone happened to see the murderer leaving the office, he had to be able to say he had gone in to look for Heller and Heller wasn't there, and he couldn't if the body was there in sight. There are marks on the floor where the body—and Heller was a featherweight—was dragged to the closet. In leaving, he left the door ajar, to make it more plausible, if someone saw him, that he had found it that way. Also—"

"Fallacy."

"I'll tell him you said so the first chance I get. Also, of course, he couldn't leave the building. Knowing that Heller started to see callers at eleven o'clock, those people had all come early so as not to have a long wait. Including the murderer. He had to go to the waiting room and wait with the others. One of them did leave, the nurse, and she made a point of telling Goodwin why she was going, and it's up to her to make it stick under questioning."

"You were going to connect me with a crime."

"Right." Cramer was positive. "First one more fact. The gun was in the closet with the body, under it on the floor. It's an old Gustein flug, a nasty little short-nose, and there's not a chance in a thousand of tracing it, though we're trying. Now here are my assumptions. The murderer went armed to kill, pushed the button at the door of Heller's office, and was admitted. Since Heller went to his desk and sat, he couldn't—"

"Established?"

"Yes. He couldn't have been in fear of a mortal attack. But after some conversation, which couldn't have been more than a few minutes on account of the timetable as verified, he was not only in fear, he felt that death was upon him, and in that super-soundproofed room he was helpless. The gun had been drawn and was aimed at him. He knew it was all up. He talked, trying to stall, not because he had any hope of living, but because he wanted to leave a message to be read after he was dead. Shaking with nervousness, with a trembling hand, perhaps a pleading one, he upset the jar of pencils on his desk, and then he nervously fumbled with them, moving them around on the desk in front of him, all the while talking. Then the gun went off, and he wasn't nervous any more. The murderer circled the desk, made sure his victim was dead, and dragged the body to the closet. It didn't occur to him that the scattered pencils had been arranged to convey a message—if it had, one sweep of a hand would have taken care of it. It was desperately urgent for him to get out of there and into the waiting room."

Cramer stood up. "If you'll let me have eight pencils I'll show you how they were."

Wolfe opened his desk drawer, but I got there first with a handful taken from my tray. Cramer moved around to Wolfe's side, and Wolfe, making a face, moved his chair to make room.

"I'm in Heller's place at his desk," Cramer said, "and I'm putting them as he did from where he sat." After getting the eight pencils arranged to his satisfaction, he stepped aside. "There it is, take a look."

Wolfe inspected it from his side, and I from mine. It was like this from Wolfe's side:

"You say," Wolfe inquired, "that was a message?"
"Yes," Cramer asserted. "It has to be."

"By mandate? Yours?"

"Blah. You know damn well there's not one chance in a million those pencils took that pattern by accident. Goodwin, you saw them. Were they like that?"

"Approximately," I conceded. "I didn't know there was a corpse in the closet at the time, so I wasn't as interested in it as you were. But since you ask me, the pencil points were not all in the same direction, and an eraser from one of them was there in the middle." I put a fingertip on the spot. "Right there."

"Fix it as you saw it."

I went around and joined them at Wolfe's side of the desk and did as requested, removing an eraser from one of the pencils and placing it as I had indicated. Then it was like this:

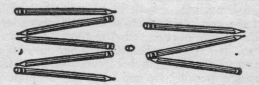

"Of course," I said, "you had the photographer shoot it. I don't say that's exact, but they were pointing in different directions, and the eraser was there."

"Didn't you realize it was a message?"

"Nuts. Someday you'll set a trap that'll catch me, and I'll snarl. Sure, I thought it was Heller's way of telling me he had gone to the bathroom and would be back in eight minutes. Eight pencils, see? Pretty clever. Isn't that how you read it?"

"It is not." Cramer was emphatic. "I think Heller turned it sideways to make it less likely that his attacker would see what it was. Move around here, please. Both of you. Look at it from here."

Wolfe and I joined him at the left end of the desk and looked as requested. One glance was enough. You can see what we saw by turning the page a quarter-turn counterclockwise.

Cramer spoke. "Could you ask for a plainer NW?"

"I could," I objected. "Why the extra pencil on the left of the W?"

"He put it there deliberately, for camouflage, to make it less obvious, or it rolled there accidentally, I don't care which. It is unmistakably NW." He focused on Wolfe. "I promised to connect you with a crime."

Wolfe, back in his chair, interlaced his fingers. "You're not serious."

"The hell I'm not." Cramer returned to the red leather chair and sat. "That's why I came here, and came alone. You deny you sent Goodwin there, but I don't believe you. He admits he was in Heller's office ten minutes, because he has to, since the doorman saw him go up and five people saw him enter the waiting room. In a drawer of Heller's desk is an envelope addressed to you, containing five hundred dollars in cash. But the clincher is that message. Heller, seated at his desk, sure that he is going to be killed in a matter of seconds, uses those seconds to leave a message. Can there be any question what the message was about? Not for me. It was about the person or persons responsible for his death. I am assuming that its purpose was to identify that person or persons. Do you reject that assumption?"

"No. I think it quite likely. Highly probable."

"You admit it?"

"I don't admit it, I state it."

"Then I ask you to suggest any person or persons other than you whom the initials NW might identify. Unless you can do that here and now I'm going to take you and Goodwin downtown as material witnesses. I've got men in cars outside. If I didn't do it the DA would."

Wolfe straightened up and sighed deep, clear down. "You are being uncommonly obnoxious, Mr. Cramer." He got to his feet. "Excuse me a moment." Detouring around Cramer's feet, he crossed to the other side of the room, to the bookshelves back of the big globe, reached up to a high one, took a book down, and opened it. He was too far away for me to see what it was. He turned first to the back of the book, where the index would be if it had one, and then to a page near the middle of it. He went on to another page, and another, while Cramer, containing his emotions under pressure, got a cigar from a pocket, stuck it in his mouth and sank his teeth in it. He never lit one.

Finally Wolfe returned to his desk, opened a drawer and put the book in it, and closed and locked the drawer. Cramer was speaking. "I'm not being fantastic. You didn't kill him; you weren't there. I'm not even assuming Goodwin killed him, though he could have. I'm saying that Heller left a message that would give a lead to the killer, and the message says NW, and that stands for Nero Wolfe, and therefore you know something, and I want to know what. I want a yes or no to this. Do you or do you not know something that indicates, or may indicate, who murdered Leo Heller?"

Wolfe, settled in his chair again, nodded. "Yes."

"Ah. You do. What?"

"The message he left."

"The message only says NW. Go on from there."

"I need more information. I need to know—are the pencils still there on his desk as you found them?"

"Yes. They haven't been disturbed."

"You have a man there, of course. Get him on the phone and let me talk to him. You will hear us."

Cramer hesitated, not liking it, then decided he might as well string along, came to my desk, dialed a number, got his man, and told him Wolfe would speak to him. Wolfe took it with his phone while Cramer stayed at mine.

Wolfe was courteous but crisp. "I understand those pencils are there on the desk as they were found, that all but one of them have erasers in their ends, and that an eraser is there on the desk, between the two groups of pencils. Is that correct?"

"Right." The dick sounded bored. I was getting it from the phone on the table over by the globe.

"Take the eraser and insert it in the end of the pencil that hasn't one in it. I want to know if the eraser was loose enough to slip out accidentally."

"Inspector, are you on? You said not to disturb—"

"Go ahead," Cramer growled. "I'm right here."

"Yes, sir. Hold it, please."

There was a long wait, and then he was back on. "The eraser couldn't have slipped out accidentaly. Part of it is still clamped in the end of the pencil. It had to be pulled out, torn apart, and the torn surfaces are bright and fresh.

I can pull one out of another pencil and tell you how much force it takes."

"No, thank you, that's all I need. But to make certain, and for the record, I suggest that you send the pencil and eraser to the laboratory to check that the torn surfaces fit."

"Do I do that, Inspector?"

"Yeah, you might as well. Mark them properly."

"Yes, sir."

Cramer returned to the red leather chair, and I went to mine. He tilted the cigar upward from the corner of his mouth and demanded, "So what?"

"You know quite well what," Wolfe declared. "The eraser was yanked out and placed purposely, and was a part of the message. No doubt as a dot after the N to show it was an initial? And he was interrupted permanently before he could put one after the W?"

"Sarcasm don't change it any. It's still NW."

"No. It isn't. It never was."

"For me and the district attorney it is. I guess we'd better get on down to his office."

Wolfe upturned a palm. "There you are. You're not hare-brained, but you are pigheaded. I warn you, sir, that if you proceed on the assumption that Mr. Heller's message says NW, you are doomed; the best you can expect is to be tagged a jackass."

"I suppose you know what it does say."

"Yes."

"You do?"

"Yes."

"I'm waiting."

"You'll continue to wait. If I thought I could earn this money"—Wolfe tapped his pocket—"by deciphering that message for you, that would be simple, but in your present state of mind you would only think I was contriving a humbug."

"Try me."

"No, sir." Wolfe half closed his eyes. "An alternative. You can go on as you have started and see where it lands you, understanding that Mr. Goodwin and I will persistently deny any knowledge of the affair or those concerned in it except what has been given you, and I'll pursue my own course; or you can bring the murderer here and let me at him—with you present."

"I'll be glad to. Name him."

"When I find him. I need all six of them, to learn which one Heller's message identifies. Since I can translate the message and you can't, you need me more than I need you, but you can save me much time and trouble and expense."

Cramer's level gaze had no trace whatever of affection or sympathy. "If you can translate that message and refuse to disclose it, you're withholding evidence."

"Nonsense. A conjecture is not evidence. Heaven knows your conjecture that it says NW isn't. Nor is mine, but it should lead to some if I do the leading." Wolfe flung a hand impatiently, and his voice rose. "Confound it, am I suggesting a gambol for my refreshment? Do you think I welcome an invasion of my premises by platoons of policemen herding a drove of scared and suspected citizens?"

"No. I know damn well you don't." Cramer took the cigar from his mouth and regarded it as if trying to decide exactly what it was. That accomplished, he glanced at Wolfe and then looked at me, by no means as a bosom friend.

"I'll use the phone," he said, and got up and came to my desk.

4

With three of the six scared citizens, it was a good thing that Wolfe didn't have to start from scratch. They had been absolutely determined not to tell why they had gone to see Leo Heller, and, as we learned from the transcripts of interviews and copies of statements they had signed, the cops had had a time dragging it out of them.

By the time the first one was brought to us in the office, a little after eight o'clock, Wolfe had sort of resigned himself to personal misery and was bravely facing it. Not only had he had to devour his dinner in one-fourth the usual time; also he had been compelled to break one of his strictest rules and read documents while eating—and all that in the company of Inspector Cramer, who had accepted an invitation to have a bite. Of course Cramer returned to the office with us and called in, from the assemblage in the front room, a police stenographer, who settled himself in a chair at the end of my desk. Sergeant Purley Stebbins, who once in a spasm of generosity admitted that he couldn't prove I was a hoodlum, after bringing the citizen in and seating him facing Wolfe and Cramer, took a chair against the wall.

The citizen, whose name as furnished by the documents was John R. Winslow, was the big guy in a dark blue topcoat and homburg who had stuck his head out of the elevator for a look at Archie Goodwin. He now looked unhappy and badly wilted, and was one of the three who had tried to refuse to tell what he had gone to Heller for; and considering what it was I couldn't blame him much.

He started in complaining. "I think—I think this is unconstitutional. The police have forced me to tell about my private affairs, and maybe that couldn't be helped, but Nero Wolfe is a private detective, and I don't have to submit to questioning by him."

"I'm here," Cramer said. "I can repeat Wolfe's questions if you insist, but it will take more time."

"Suppose," Wolfe suggested, "we start and see how it goes. I've read your statement, Mr. Winslow, and I—"

"You had no right to! They had no right to let you! They promised me it would be confidential unless it had to be used as evidence!"

"Please, Mr. Winslow, don't bounce up like that. A hysterical woman is bad enough, but a hysterical man is insufferable. I assure you I am as discreet as any policeman. According to your statement, today was your third visit to Mr. Heller's office. You were trying to supply him with enough information for him to devise a formula for determining how much longer your aunt will live. You expect to inherit a considerable fortune from her, and you wanted to make plans intelligently based on reasonable expectations. So you say, but reports are being received which indicate that you are deeply in debt and are hard pressed. Do you deny that?"

"No." Winslow's jaw worked. "I don't deny it."

"Are your debts, or any part of them, connected with any violation of the law? Any criminal act?"

"No!"

"Granted that Mr. Heller could furnish a valid calculation on your aunt's life, how would that help you any?"

Winslow looked at Cramer and met only a stony stare. He went back to Wolfe. "I was negotiating to borrow a very large sum against my—expectations. There was to be a certain percentage added for each month that passed before repayment was made, and I had to know what my chances were. It was a question of probabilities, and I went to an expert."

"What data had you given Heller as a basis for his calculations?"

"My God, I couldn't—all kinds of things."

"For instance?" Wolfe insisted.

Winslow looked at the police stenographer and me, but we couldn't help. He returned to Wolfe. "Hundreds of things. My aunt's age, her habits—eating, sleeping, everything I could—her health as far as I knew about it, the ages of her parents and grandparents when they died, her weight and build—I gave him photographs—her activities and interests, her temperament, her attitude to doctors, her politics—"

"Politics?"

"Yes. Heller said her pleasure or pain at the election of Eisenhower was a longevity factor."

Wolfe grunted. "The claptrap of the charlatan. Did he also consider as a longevity factor the possibility that you might intervene by dispatching your aunt?"

That struck Winslow as funny. He did not guffaw, but he tittered, and it did not suit his build. Wolfe insisted, "Did he?"

"I really don't know, really." Winslow tittered again.

"From whom did your aunt inherit her fortune?"

"Her husband. My Uncle Norton."

"When did he die?"

"Six years ago. In nineteen forty-seven."

"How? Of what?"

"He was shot accidentally while hunting. Hunting deer."

"Were you present?"

"Not present, no. I was more than a mile away at the time."

"Did you get a legacy from him?"

"No." Some emotion was mobilizing Winslow's blood and turning his face pink. "He sneered at me. He left me six cents in his will. He didn't like me."

Wolfe turned to speak to Cramer, but the inspector forestalled him. "Two men are already on it. The shooting accident was up in Maine."

"I would like to say how I feel about this," Winslow told them. "I mean the questions that have been asked me about my uncle's death. I regard them as a compliment. They assume that I might have been capable of shooting my uncle, and that is a very high compliment, and you say there are two men on it, so it is being investigated, and that is a compliment too. My aunt would be amused at the idea of my having killed Uncle Norton, and she would be amused at the idea that I might try to kill her. I wouldn't mind a bit having her know about that, but if she finds out what I went to Leo Heller for—God help me." He gestured in appeal. "I was promised, absolutely promised."

"We disclose people's private affairs," Cramer rumbled, "only when it is unavoidable."

Wolfe was pouring beer. When the foam was at the rim he put the bottle down and resumed. "I have promised nothing, Mr. Winslow, but I have no time for tattle. Here's a suggestion. You're in this pickle only because of your association with Mr. Heller, and the question is, was there anything in that association to justify this badgering? Suppose you tell us. Start at the beginning, and recall as well as you can every word that passed between you. Go right through it. I'll interrupt as little as possible."

"You've already seen it," Cramer objected. "The transcript, the statement—what the hell, have you got a lead or haven't you?"

Wolfe nodded. "We have a night for it," he said, not happily. "Mr. Winslow doesn't know what the lead is, and it's Greek to you." He went to Winslow. "Go ahead, sir. Everything that you said to Mr. Heller, and everything he said to you."

It took more than an hour, including interruptions. The interruptions came from various city employees who were scattered around the house—the front room, the dining room, and three upstairs bedrooms—working on other scared citizens, and from the telephone. Two of the phone calls were from homicide dicks who were trying to locate a citizen who had got mislaid—one named Henrietta Tillotson, Mrs. Albert Tillotson, the overfed matron whom I had seen in Heller's waiting room with the others. There were also calls from the police commissioner and the DA's office and other interested parties.

When Purley Stebbins got up to escort Winslow from the room, Wolfe's lead was still apparently Greek to Cramer, as it was to me. As the door closed behind them Cramer spoke emphatically. "I think it's a goddam farce. I think that message was NW, meaning you, and you're stalling for some kind of a play."

"And if so?" Wolfe was testy. "Why are you tolerating this? Because if the message did mean me I'm the crux, and your only alternative is to cart me downtown, and that would merely make me mum, and you know it." He drank beer and put the glass down. "However, maybe we can expedite it without too great a risk. Tell your men who are now interviewing these people to be alert for something connected with the figure six. They must give no hint of it, they must themselves not mention it, but if the figure six appears in any segment of the interview they should concentrate on that segment until it is exhausted. They all know, I presume, of Heller's suspicion that one of his clients had committed a serious crime?"

"They know that Goodwin says so. What's this about six?"

Wolfe shook his head. "That will have to do. Even that may be foolhardy, since they're your men, not mine."

"Winslow's uncle died six years ago and left him six cents."

"I'm quite aware of it. You say that is being investigated. Do you want Mr. Goodwin to pass this word?"

Cramer said no thanks, he would, and left the room.

By the time he returned, citizen number two had been brought in by Stebbins, introduced to Wolfe, and seated where Winslow had been. She was Susan Maturo. She looked fully as harassed as she had that morning, but I wouldn't say much more so. There was now, of course, a new aspect to the matter: did she look harassed or guilty? She was undeniably attractive, but so had Maude Vail been, and she had poisoned two husbands. There was the consideration that if Heller had been killed by the client whom he suspected of having committed a crime, it must have been a client he had seen previously at least once, or how could he have got grounds for a suspicion; and, according to Susan Maturo, she had never called on Heller before and had never seen him. But actually that eliminated neither her nor Agatha Abbey, who also claimed that that morning had been her first visit. It was known that Heller had sometimes made engagements by telephone to meet prospective clients elsewhere, and Miss Maturo and Miss Abbey might well have been among that number.

Opening up on her, Wolfe was not too belligerent, probably because she had accepted an offer of beer and, after drinking some, had licked her lips. It pleases him when people share his joys.

"You are aware, Miss Maturo," he told her, "that you are in a class by yourself. The evidence indicates that Mr. Heller was killed by one of the six people who entered that building this morning to call on him, and you are the only one of the six who departed before eleven o'clock, Mr. Heller's appointment hour. Your explanation of your departure as given in your statement is close to incoherent. Can't you improve on it?"

She looked at me. I did not throw her a kiss, but neither did I glower. "I've reported what you told me," I assured her, "exactly as you said it."

She nodded at me vaguely and turned to Wolfe. "Do I have to go through it again?"

"You will probably," Wolfe advised her, "have to go through it again a dozen times. Why did you leave?"

She gulped, started to speak, found no sound was coming out, and had to start over again. "You know about the explosion and fire at the Montrose Hospital a month ago?"

"Certainly. I read newspapers."

"You know that three hundred and two people died there that night. I was there working, in Ward G on the sixth floor. In addition to those who died, many were injured, but I went all through it and I didn't get a scratch or any burn. My dearest friend was killed, burned to death trying to save the patients, and another dear friend is crippled for life, and a young doctor I was engaged to marry—he was killed in the explosion, and others I knew. I don't know how I came out of it without a mark, because I'm sure I tried to help. I'm positively sure of that, but I did, and that's one trouble, I guess, because I couldn't be glad about it—how could I?"

She seemed to expect an answer, so Wolfe muttered, "No. Not to be expected."

"I am not," she said, "the kind of person who hates people."

She stopped, so Wolfe said, "No?"

"No, I'm not. I never have been. But I began to hate the man—or if it was a woman, I don't care which—that put the bomb there and did it. I can't say I went out of my mind because I don't think I did, but that's how I felt. After two weeks I tried to go back to work at another hospital, but I couldn't. I read all there was in the newspapers, hoping they would catch him, and I couldn't think of anything else, and I dreamed about it every night, and I went to the police and wanted to help, but of course they had already questioned me and I had told everything I knew. The days went by, and it looked as if they never would catch him, and I wanted to do something, and I had read about that Leo Heller, and I decided to go to him and get him to do it."

Wolfe made a noise and her head jerked up. "I said I hated him!"

Wolfe nodded. "So you did. Go on."

"And I went, that's all. I had some money saved, and I could borrow some, to pay him. But while I was sitting there in the waiting room, with that man and woman there, I suddenly thought I must be crazy, I must have got so bitter and vindictive I didn't realize what I was doing, and I wanted to think about it, and I got up and went. Going down in the elevator I felt as if a crisis had passed —that's a feeling a nurse often has about other people— and then as I left the elevator I heard the names Archie Goodwin and Nero Wolfe, and the idea came to me, why not get them to find him? So I spoke to Mr. Goodwin, and there I was again, but I couldn't make myself tell him about it, so I just told him I wanted to see Nero Wolfe to ask his advice, and he said he would try to arrange it, and he would phone me or I could phone him."

She fluttered a hand. "That's how it was."

Wolfe regarded her. "It's not incoherent, but neither is it sapient. Do you consider yourself an intelligent woman?"

"Why—yes. Enough to get along. I'm a good nurse, and a good nurse has to be intelligent."

"Yet you thought that quack could expose the man who planted the bomb in the hospital by his hocus-pocus?"

"I thought he did it scientifically. I knew he had a great reputation, just as you have."

"Good heavens." Wolfe opened his eyes wide at her. "It is indeed a bubble, as Jacques said. What were you going to ask my advice about?"

"Whether you thought there was any chance—whether you thought the police were going to find him."

Wolfe's eyes were back to normal, half shut again. "This performance I'm engaged in, Miss Maturo—this inquisition of a person involved by circumstance in a murder—is a hubbub in a jungle, at least in its preliminary stage. Blind, I grope, and proceed by feel. You say you never saw Mr. Heller, but you can't prove it. I am free to assume that you had seen him, not at his office, and talked with him; that you were convinced, no matter how, that he had planted the bomb in the hospital and caused the holocaust; and that, moved by an obsessive rancor, you went to his place and killed him. One ad—"

She was gawking. "Why on earth would I think he had planted the bomb?"

"I have no idea. As I said, I'm groping. One advantage of that assumption would be that you have confessed to a hatred so overpowering that surely it might have impelled you to kill if and when you identified its object. It is Mr. Cramer, not I, who is deploying the hosts of justice in this enterprise, but no doubt two or three men are calling on your friends and acquaintances to learn if you have ever hinted a suspicion of Leo Heller in connection with the hospital disaster. Also they are probably asking whether you had any grudge against the hospital that might have provoked you to plant the bomb yourself."

"My God!" A muscle at the side of her neck was twitching. "Me? Is that what it's like?"

"It is indeed. That wouldn't be incongruous. Your proclaimed abhorrence of the perpetrator could be simply the screeching of your remorse."

"Well, it isn't." Suddenly she was out of her chair, and a bound took her to Wolfe's desk, and her palms did a tattoo on the desk as she leaned forward at him. "Don't you dare say a thing like that! The six people I cared for most in the world—they all died that night! How would you feel?" More tattoo. "How would anybody feel?"

I was up and at her elbow, but no bodily discipline was required. She straightened and for a moment stood trembling all over, then got her control back and went to her chair and sat. "I'm sorry," she said in a tight little voice.

"You should be," Wolfe said grimly. A woman cutting loose is always too much for him. "Pounding the top of my desk settles nothing. What were the names of the six people you cared for most in the world, who died?"

She told him, and he wanted to know more about them. I was beginning to suspect that actually he had no more of a lead than I did, that he had given Cramer a runaround to jostle him loose from the NW he had fixed on, and that, having impulsively impounded the five hundred bucks, he had decided to spend the night trying to earn it. The line he now took with Susan Maturo bore me out. It was merely the old grab-bag game—keep her talking, about anything and anybody, in the hope that she would spill something that would faintly resemble a straw. I had known Wolfe, when the pickings had been extremely slim, to play that game for hours on end.

He was still at it with Susan Maturo when an individual entered with a message for Cramer which he delivered in a whisper. Cramer got up and started for the door, then thought better of it and turned.

"You might as well be in on this," he told Wolfe. "They've got Mrs. Tillotson, and she's here."

That was a break for Susan Maturo, since Wolfe might have kept her going another hour or so, though I suppose all it got her was an escort to some lieutenant or sergeant in another room, who started at her all over again. As she arose to go she favored me with a glance. It looked as if she intended it for a smile to show there were no hard feelings, but if so it was the poorest excuse for a smile I had ever seen. If it hadn't been unprofessional I would have gone and given her a pat on the shoulder.

The newcomer who was ushered in was not Mrs. Tillot-

son but an officer of the law, not in uniform. He was one
of the newer acquisitions on Homicide, and I had never
seen him before, but I admired his manly stride as he approached and his snappy stance when he halted and faced
Cramer, waiting to be spoken to.

"Who did you leave over there?" Cramer asked him.

"Murphy, sir. Timothy Murphy."

"Okay. You tell it. Hold it." Cramer turned to Wolfe.
"This man's name is Roca. He was on post at Heller's place.
It was him you asked about the pencils and the eraser. Go
on, Roca."

"Yes, sir. The doorman in the lobby phoned up that
there was a woman down there that wanted to come up,
and I told him to let her come. I thought that was com-
patible."

"You did."

"Yes, sir."

"Then go ahead."

"She came up in the elevator. She wouldn't tell me her
name. She asked me questions about how much longer
would I be there and did I expect anybody else to come,
and so on. We bantered back and forth, my objective being
to find out who she was, and then she came right out with
it. She took a roll of bills from her bag. She offered me
three hundred dollars, and then four hundred, and finally
five hundred, if I would unlock the cabinets in Heller's
office and let her be in there alone for an hour. That put
me in a quandary."

"It did."

"Yes, sir."

"How did you get out?"

"If I had had keys to the cabinets I would have accepted
her offer. I would have unlocked them and left her in there.
When she was ready to go I would have arrested her and
taken her to be searched, and we would have known what
she had taken from the cabinet. That would have broken
the case. But I had no keys to the cabinets."

"Uh-huh. If you had had keys and had unlocked the
cabinets and left her in there, and she had taken something
from a cabinet and burned it up, you would have collected
the ashes and sent them to the laboratory for examination
by modern scientific methods."

Roca swallowed. "I admit I didn't think about burning. But if I had had keys I would have thought harder."

"I bet you would. Did you take her money for evidence?"

"No, sir. I thought that might be instigation. I took her into custody. I phoned in. When a relief came, I brought her here to you. I am staying here to face her."

"You've faced her enough for tonight. Plenty. We'll have a talk later. Go and tell Burger to bring her in."

5

Although my stay in Heller's waiting room that morning had been brief, I have long been trained to see what I look at and to remember what I see, and I would hardly have recognized Mrs. Albert Tillotson. She had lost five pounds and gained twice that many wrinkles, and the contrast between her lipstick and her drained-out skin made her look more like a woman-hater's pin-up than an overfed matron.

"I wish to speak with you privately," she told Inspector Cramer.

She was one of those. Her husband was president of something, and therefore it was absurd to suppose that she was not to expect privileges. It took Cramer a good five minutes to get it into her head that she was just one of the girls, and it was such a shock that she had to take time out to decide how to react to it.

She decided on a barefaced lie. She demanded to know if the man who had brought her there was a member of the police force, and Cramer replied that he was.

"Well," she declared, "he shouldn't be. You may know that late this afternoon a police officer called at my residence to see me. He told me that Leo Heller had been killed, murdered, and wanted to know for what purpose I had gone to his office this morning. Naturally I didn't want to be involved in an ugly thing like that, so I told him I hadn't gone to see Leo Heller, but he convinced me that that wouldn't do, so I said I had gone to see him, but on an intimate personal matter that I wouldn't tell—Is that man putting down what I'm saying?"

"Yes. That's his job."

"I wouldn't want it. Nor yours either. The officer insisted that I must tell why I had gone to see that Heller, and I refused, and he insisted, and I refused. When he said he would have to take me to the district attorney's office, under arrest if necessary, and I saw that he meant it, I told him. I told him that my husband and I have been having some difficulty with our son, especially his schooling, and I went to Heller to ask what college would be best for him. I answered the officer's questions, within reason, and finally he left. Perhaps you knew all this."

Cramer nodded. "Yes."

"Well, after the officer had gone I began to worry, and I went to see a friend and ask her advice. The trouble was that I had given Heller many details about my son, some of them very intimate and confidential, and since he had been murdered the police would probably go through all his papers, and those details were private and I wanted to keep them private. I knew that Heller had made all his notes in a personal shorthand that no one else could read —anyhow he had said so, but I couldn't be sure, and it was very important. After I had discussed it with my friend a long time, for hours, I decided to go to Heller's place and ask whoever was in charge to let me have any papers relating to my family affairs, since they were not connected with the murder."

"I see," Cramer assured her.

"And that's what I did. And the officer there pretended to listen to me, he pretended to be agreeing with me, and then suddenly he arrested me for trying to bribe an officer; and when I indignantly denied it, as of course I did, and started to leave, he detained me by force, and he actually was going to put handcuffs on me! So I came with him, and here I am, and I hope you realize I have a complaint to make and I am making it!"

Cramer was eying her. "Did you try to bribe him?"

"No, I didn't!"

"You didn't offer him money?"

"No!"

Purley Stebbins permitted a low sound, half growl and half snort, to escape him. Cramer, ignoring that impertinence from a subordinate, took a deep breath and let it out again.

"Shall I take it?" Wolfe inquired.

"No, thank you," Cramer said acidly. He was keeping his eyes at Mrs. Tillotson. "You're making a mistake, madam," he told her. "All these lies don't do you any good. They just make it harder for you. Try telling the truth for a change."

She drew herself up, but it wasn't very impressive because she was pretty well fagged after her hard day. "You're calling me a liar," she accused Cramer, "and in front of witnesses." She pointed a finger at the police stenographer. "You get that down just the way he said it!"

"He will," Cramer assured her. "Look, Mrs. Tillotson. You admit you lied about going to see Heller until you saw it wouldn't work, when you realized that the doorman would swear that you were there not only this morning but also previously. Now about your trying to bribe an officer. That's a felony. If we charge you with it, and you go to trial, I can't say who the jury will believe, you or the officer, but I know who I believe. I believe him, and you're lying about it."

"Get him in here," she challenged. "I want to face him."

"He wants to face you too, but that wouldn't help any. I'm satisfied that you're lying, and also that you're lying about what you wanted to get from Heller's files. He made his notes in a private code that it will take a squad of experts to decipher, and you knew that, and I do not believe that you took the risk of going there and trying to bribe an officer just to get his notes about you and your family. I believe there is something in his files that can easily be recoginzed as pertaining to you or your family, and that's what you were after. In the morning we'll have men going through the contents of the files, item by item, and if anything like that is there they'll spot it. Meanwhile I'm holding you for further questioning about your attempt to bribe an officer. If you want to telephone a lawyer, you may—one phone call, with an officer present."

Cramer's head swiveled. "Stebbins, take her in to Lieutenant Rowcliff, and tell Rowcliff how it stands."

Purley arose. Mrs. Tillotson was shrinkng, looking less overfed every second, right in front of our eyes. "Will you wait a minute?" she demanded.

"Two minutes, madam. But don't try cooking up any more lies. You're no good at it."

"That man misunderstood me. I wasn't trying to bribe him."

"I said you may phone a lawyer—"

"I don't want a lawyer." She was sure about that. "If they go through those files they'll find what I was after, so I might as well tell you. It's some letters in envelopes addressed to me. They're not signed, they're anonymous, and I wanted that Heller to find out who sent them."

"Are they about your son?"

"No. They're about me. They threaten me with something, and I was sure it was leading up to blackmail."

"How many letters?"

"Six."

"What do they threaten you with?"

"They—they don't exactly threaten. They're quotations from things. One of them says, 'He that cannot pay, let him pray.' Another one says, 'He that dies pays all debts.' Another one says, 'So comes a reckoning when the banquet's o'er.' The others are longer, but that's what they're like."

"What made you think they were leading up to blackmail?"

"Wouldn't you? 'He that cannot pay, let him pray.'"

"And you wanted Heller to identify the sender. How many times had you seen him?"

"Twice."

"Of course you had given him all the information you could. We'll get the letters in the morning, but you can tell us now what you told Heller. As far as possible, everything that was said by both of you."

I permitted myself to grin, not discreetly, and glanced at Wolfe to see if he was properly appreciative of Cramer's adopting his approach, but he was just sitting there looking patient.

It was hard to tell, for me at least, how much Mrs. Tillotson was giving and how much she was covering. If there was something in her past that someone might have felt she should pay for or give a reckoning of, either she didn't know what it was, or she had kept it from Heller, or she had told him but certainly didn't intend to let us in on it. It went on and on, with her concentrating hard on remembering her conversations with Heller and all the data she had given him for factors of his formulas, and with Cramer playing her back and forth until she was so tied up in contradictions that it would have taken a dozen mathematical wizards to make head or tail of it.

Wolfe finally intervened. He glanced up at the wall clock, shifted in his chair to get his seventh of a ton bearing on another spot, and announced, "It's after midnight. Thank heaven you have an army to start sorting this out and checking it. If your Lieutenant Rowcliff is still here, let him have her, and let's have some cheese. I'm hungry."

Cramer, as ready for a recess as anybody, had no objection. Purley Stebbins removed Mrs. Tillotson. The stenographer went on a private errand. I went to the kitchen to give Fritz a hand, knowing that he was running himself ragged furnishing trays of sandwiches to flocks of Homicide personnel distributed all over the premises. When I returned to the office with a supply of provender, Cramer was riding Wolfe, pouring it on, and Wolfe was leaning back in his chair with his eyes shut. I passed around plates of Fritz's *il pesto* and crackers, with beer for Wolfe and the stenographer, coffee for Cramer and Stebbins, and milk for me.

In four minutes Cramer inquired, "What is this stuff?"

Wolfe told him. "*Il pesto.*"

"What's in it?"

"Canestrato cheese, anchovies, pig liver, black walnuts, chives, sweet basil, garlic, and olive oil."

"Good God."

In another four minutes Cramer addressed me in the tone of one doing a gracious favor. "I'll take some more of that, Goodwin."

But while I was gathering the empty plates he started in on Wolfe again. Wolfe didn't bother to counter. He waited until Cramer halted for breath and then growled, "It's nearly one o'clock, and we have three more."

Cramer sent Purley for another scared citizen. This time it was the thin tall bony specimen who, entering the lobby on Thirty-seventh Street that morning, had stopped to aim a rude stare at Susan Maturo and me seated on the bench by the fireplace. Having read his statement, I now knew that his name was Jack Ennis, that he was an expert diemaker, at present unemployed, that he was unmarried, that he lived in Queens, and that he was a born inventor who had not yet cashed in. His brown suit had not been pressed.

When Cramer told him that questions from Wolfe were to be considered a part of the official inquiry into Leo Heller's death, Ennis cocked his head to appraise Wolfe, as if deciding whether or not such a procedure deserved his okay.

"You're a self-made man," he told Wolfe. "I've read about you. How old are you?"

Wolfe returned his gaze. "Some other time, Mr. Ennis. Tonight you're the target, not me. You're thirty-eight, aren't you?"

Ennis smiled. He had a wide mouth with thin colorless lips, and his smile wasn't especially attractive. "Excuse me if you thought I was being fresh, asking how old you are, but I don't really give a damn. I know you're right at the top of your racket, and I wondered how long it took you to get started up. I'm going to the top too, before I'm through, but it's taking me a hell of a time to get a start, and I wondered about you. How old were you when you first got your name in the paper?"

"Two days. A notice of my birth. I understand that your call on Leo Heller was connected with your determination to get a start as an inventor?"

"That's right." Ennis smiled again. "Look. This is all a lot of crap. The cops have been at me now for seven hours, and where are they? What's the sense in going on with it? Why in the name of God would I want to kill that guy?"

"That's what I'd like to know."

"Well, search me. I've got patents on six inventions, and none of them is on the market. One of them is not perfect—I know damn well it's not—but it needs only one more trick to make it an absolute whiz. I can't find the trick. I've read about this Heller, and it seemed to me that if I gave him all the dope, all the stuff he needed for one of his formulas, there was a good chance he would come up with the answer. So I went to him. I spent three long sessions with him. He finally thought he had enough to try to work up a formula, and he was taking a crack at it, and I had a date to see him this morning and find out how it was going."

Ennis stopped for emphasis. "So I'm hoping. After all the sweating I've done and the dough I've spent, maybe I'm going to get it at last. So I go. I go upstairs to his office and shoot him dead, and then I go to the waiting room and sit down and wait." He smiled. "Listen. If you want to say there are smarter men than me, I won't argue. Maybe you're smarter yourself. But I'm not a lunatic, am I?"

Wolfe's lips were pursed. "I won't commit myself on that, Mr. Ennis. But you have by no means demonstrated that it is fatuous to suppose you might have killed Heller. What if he devised a formula from the data you supplied, discovered the trick that would transform your faulty contraption into a whiz, as you expressed it, and refused to divulge it except on intolerable terms? That would be a magnificent motive for murder."

"It sure would," Ennis agreed without reservation. "I would have killed him with pleasure." He leaned forward and was suddenly intense and in dead earnest. "Look. I'm headed for the top. I've got what I need in here"—he tapped his forehead—"and nothing and nobody is going to stop me. If Heller had done what you said, I might have killed him, I don't deny it; but he didn't." He jerked to Cramer. "And I'm glad of a chance to tell you what I've told those bozos that have been grilling me. I want to go through Heller's papers to see if I can find the formula he worked up for me. Maybe I can't recognize it, and if I do I doubt if I can figure it out, but I want to look for it, and not next year either."

"We're doing the looking," Cramer said dryly. "If we find anything that can be identified as relating to you, you'll see it, and eventually you may get it."

"I don't want it eventually, I want it now. Do you know how long I've been working on that thing? Four years! It's mine, you understand that, it's mine!" He was getting upset.

"Calm down, bud," Cramer advised him. "We're right with you in seeing to it that you get what's yours."

"Meanwhile," Wolfe said, "there's a point or two. When

you entered that building this morning, why did you stop
and gape at Mr. Goodwin and Miss Maturo?"

Ennis's chin went up. "Who says I did?"

"I do, on information. Archie. Did he?"

"Yes," I stated. "Rudely."

"Well," Ennis told Wolfe, "he's bigger than I am.
Maybe I did, at that."

"Why? Any special reason?"

"It depends on what you call special. I thought I recognized her, a girl I knew once, and then saw I was wrong.
She was much too young."

"Very well. I would like to explore my suggestion, which
you reject, that Heller was trying to chouse you out of
your invention as perfected by his calculations. I want
you to describe the invention as you described it to him,
particularly the flaw which you had tried so persistently
to rectify."

I won't attempt to report what followed, and I couldn't
anyhow, since I understood less than a tenth of it. I did
gather that the invention was a gadget intended to supersede all existing X-ray machines, but beyond that I got lost
in a wilderness of cathodes and atomicity and coulombs,
and if you ask me, Wolfe and Cramer were no better off.
If talking like a character out of space-science fiction proves
you're an inventor, that bird was certainly one. He stood
up to make motions to illustrate, and grabbed a pad and
pencil from Wolfe's desk to explain with drawings, and
after a while it began to look as if it would be impossible
to stop him. They finally managed it, with Sergeant Stebbins lending a hand by marching over and taking his
elbow. On his way out he turned at the door to call back,
"I want that formula, and don't you forget it!"

6

The female of an executive type was still in mink, or
rather she had it with her, but she was not so brisk. As I
said before, that morning I would have classified her as
between twenty and sixty, but the day's experiences had
worn her down closer to reality, and I would now have

put her at forty-seven. However, she was game. With all she had gone through, at that late hour she still let us know, as she deposited the mink on a chair, sat on another, crossed her legs, got out a cigarette and let me light it, and thanked me for an ashtray, that she was cool and composed and in command.

My typing her as an executive had been justified by the transcripts. Her name really was Agatha Abbey, and she was executive editor of a magazine, Mode, which I did not read regularly. After Cramer had explained the nature of the session, including Wolfe's status, Wolfe took aim and went for the center of the target.

"Miss Abbey. I presume you'd like to get to bed—I know I would—so we won't waste time flouncing around. Three things about you." He held up a finger. "First. You claim that you never saw Leo Heller. It is corroborated that you had not visited his place before today, but whether you had seen him elsewhere will be thoroughly investigated by men armed with pictures of him. They will ask people at your place of business, at your residence, and at other likely spots. If it is found that you had in fact met him and conferred with him, you won't like it."

He raised two fingers. "Second. You refused to tell why you went to see Heller. That does not brand you as a miscreant, since most people have private matters which they innocently and jealously guard, but you clung to your refusal beyond reason, even after it was explained that that information had to be given by all of the six persons who called on Heller this morning, and you were assured that it would be revealed to no one unless it proved to be an item of evidence in a murder case. You finally did give the information, but only when you perceived that if you didn't there would be a painstaking investigation into your affairs and movements."

He raised three fingers. "Third. When the information was wormed out of you, it was almost certainly flummery. You said that you wanted to engage Heller to find out who had stolen a ring from a drawer of your desk some three months ago. That was childish nonsense. I grant that even though the ring was insured you may have been intent on disclosing the culprit, and the police had failed you; but if you have enough sense to get and hold a well-paid job in a highly competitive field, as you have, surely you would have known that it was stupid to suppose Heller could help you. Even if he were not a humbug, if he were honestly applying the laws of probability to complex problems with some success, singling out a sneak thief from among a hundred possibilities was plainly an operation utterly unsuited to his technique, and even to his pretensions.'

Wolfe moved his head an inch to the left and back again. "No, Miss Abbey, it won't do. I want to know whether you saw Leo Heller before today, and in any case what you wanted of him."

The tip of her tongue had appeared four times, to flick across her lips. She spoke in a controlled, thin, steely voice. "You make it sound overwhelming, Mr. Wolfe."

"Not I. It is overwhelming."

Her sharp dark eyes went to Cramer. "You're an inspector, in charge of this business?"

"That's right."

"Do the police share Mr. Wolfe's—skepticism?"

"You can take what he said as coming from me."

"Then no matter what I tell you about why I went to see Heller, you'll investigate it? You'll check it?"

"Not necessarily. If it fits all right, and if we can't connect it with the murder, and if it's a private confidential matter, we'll let it go at that. If we do check any, we'll be careful. There are enough innocent citizens sore at us already."

Her eyes darted back to Wolfe. "What about you, Mr. Wolfe? Will you have to check?"

"I sincerely hope not. Let Mr. Cramer's assurance include me."

Her eyes went around. "What about these men?"

"They are trained confidential assistants. They hold their tongues or they lose their jobs."

The tip of her tongue came out and went in. "I'm not satisfied, but what can I do? If my only choice is between this and the whole New York detective force pawing at me, the Lord knows I take this. I phoned Leo Heller ten days ago, and he came to my office and spent two hours there. It was a business matter, not a personal one. I'm going to tell you exactly what it was, because I'm no good at ad libbing a phony. I was a damn fool to say that about the stolen ring."

She was hating it, but she went on. "You said I have sense enough to get and hold a well-paid job in a highly competitive field, but if you only knew. It's not a field, it's a corral of wild beasts. There are six female tigers trying to get their claws on my job right now, and if they all died tonight there would be six others tomorrow. If it came out what I went to Leo Heller for, that would be the finish of me."

The tip of her tongue flashed out and in. "So that's what this means to me. A magazine like *Mode* has two main functions, reporting and predicting. American women want to know what is being made and worn in Paris and New York, but even more they want to know what is going to be made and worn next season. *Mode's* reporting has been good enough—I've been all right on that—but for the past year our predictions have been utterly rotten. We've got the contacts, but something has gone haywire, and our biggest rival has made monkeys of us. Another year like that, even another season, and good-by."

Wolfe grunted. "To the magazine?"

"No, to me. So I decided to try Leo Heller. We had carried a piece about him, and I had met him. The idea was to give him everything we had—and we had plenty—about styles and colors and trends for the past ten years, and have him figure the probabilities six months ahead. He thought it was feasible, and I don't think he was a faker. He had to come to the office to go through our stuff, and of course I had to camouflage it, what he was there for, but that wasn't hard. Do you want to know what I told them he was doing?"

"I think not," Wolfe muttered.

"So he came. I phoned him the next day, and he said it would take him at least a week to determine whether he had enough information to make up a probability formula. Yesterday I phoned again, and he said he had something to discuss and asked me to call at his place this morning. I went. You know the rest of it."

She stopped. Wolfe and Cramer exchanged glances. "I would like," Wolfe said, "to have the name of the six female tigers who are after your job."

She turned white. I have never seen the color leave a face faster or more completely. "Damn you," she said in bitter fury. "So you're a rat like everybody else!"

Wolfe showed her a palm. "Please, madam. Mr. Cramer will speak for himself, but I have no desire to betray you to your enemies. I merely want—"

He saved his breath, because his audience was leaving. She got up, retrieved her mink from the other chair, draped it over her arm, turned, and headed for the door. Stebbins looked at Wolfe, Wolfe shook his head, and Stebbins trailed after her.

As he left the room at her heels, Cramer called to him, "Bring Busch!" Then he turned on Wolfe to protest. "What the hell, you had her open. Why give her a breath?"

Wolfe made a face. "The wretch. The miserable wretch. Her misogyny was already in her bones; now her misandry is too. She was dumb with rage, and it would have been futile to keep at her. But you're keeping her?"

"You're right we are. For what?" He was out of his chair, glaring down at Wolfe. "Tell me for what! Except for dragging that out of that woman, there's not one single . . ."

He was off again. I miss no opportunity of resenting Inspector Cramer—I enjoy it, and it's good for my appetite —but I must admit that on that occasion he seemed to me to have a point. I still had seen or heard no indication whatever that Wolfe's statement that he had a lead was anything but a stall, and it was half-past two in the morning, and five of them had been processed, with only one to go. So as Cramer yapped at my employer I did not cheer him on or offer him an orchid, but I had a private feeling that some of the sentiments he expressed were not positively preposterous. He was still at it when the door opened to admit Stebbins with the sixth customer.

The sergeant, after conducting this one to the seat the others had occupied, facing Wolfe and Cramer, did not go to the chair against the wall, which he had favored throughout the evening. Instead, he lowered his bulk onto one at Cramer's left, only two arms' lengths from the subject. That was interesting because it meant that he was voting for Karl Busch as his pick of the lot, and while

Stebbins had often been wrong I had known him, more than once, to be right.

Karl Busch was the slick, sly, swarthy little article with his hair pasted to his scalp. In the specifications on his transcript I had noted the key NVMS, meaning No Visible Means of Support, but that was just a nod to routine. The details of the report on him left no real doubt as to the sources he tapped for jack. He was a Broadway smoothie, third grade. He was not in the theater or sports or the flicks or any of the tough rackets, but he knew everyone who was, and as the engraved lettuce swirled around the midtown corners and got trapped in the nets of the collectors, legitimate and otherwise, he had a hundred little dodges for fastening onto a specimen for himself.

To him Cramer's tone was noticeably different. "This is Nero Wolfe," he rasped. "Answer his questions. You hear, Busch?"

Busch said he did. Wolfe, who was frowning, studying him, spoke. "Nothing is to be gained, Mr. Busch, by my starting the usual rigmarole with you. I've read your statement, and I doubt if it would be worth while to try to pester you into a contradiction. But you had three conversations with Leo Heller, and in your statement they are not reported, merely summarized. I want the details of those conversations, as completely as your memory will furnish. Start with the first one, two months ago. Exactly what was said?"

Busch slowly shook his head. "Impossible, mister."

"Word by word, no. Do your best."

"Huh-uh."

"You won't try?"

"It's this way. If I took you to the pier and ast you to try to jump across to Brooklyn, what would you do? You'd say it was impossible and why get your feet wet. That's me."

"I told you," Cramer snapped, "to answer his questions."

Busch extended a dramatic hand in appeal. "What do you want me to do, make it up?"

"I want you to do what you were told, to the best of your ability."

"Okay. This will be good. I said to him, 'Mr. Heller, my

name's Busch, and I'm a broker.' He said broker of what, and I said of anything people want broken, just for a gag, but he had no sense of humor and I saw he didn't, so I dropped that and explained. I told him there was a great demand among all kinds of people to know what horse was going to win a race the day before the race was run or even an hour before, and I had read about his line of work and was thinking that he could help to meet that demand. He said that he had thought several times about using his method on horse races, but he didn't care himself to use the method for personal bets because he wasn't a betting man, and for him to make up one of his formulas for just one race would take an awful lot of research and it would cost so much it wouldn't be worth it for any one person unless that person made a high-bracket plunge."

"You're paraphrasing it," Wolfe objected. "I'd prefer the words that were used."

"This is the best of my ability, mister."

"Very well. Go on."

"I said I wasn't a high-bracket boy myself, but anyway that wasn't here or there or under the rug, because what I had in mind was a wholesale setup. I had figgers to show him. Say he did ten races a week. I could round up at least twenty customers right off the bat. He didn't need to be any God Almighty always right; all he had to do was crack a percentage of forty or better, and it would start a fire you couldn't put out if you ran a river down it. We could have a million customers if we wanted 'em, but we wouldn't want 'em. We would hand-pick a hundred and no more, and each one would ante one C per week, which if I can add at all would make ten grand every sennight. That would—"

"What?" Wolfe exploded. "Ten grand every what?"

"Sennight."

"Meaning a week?"

"Sure."

"Where the deuce did you pick up that fine old word?"

"That's not old. Some big wit started it around last summer."

"Incredible. Go on."

"Where was— Oh, yeah. That would make half a million

little ones per year, and Heller and me would split it. Out
of my half I would expense the operating, and out of his
half he would expense the dope. He would have to walk
on his nose to cut under a hundred grand all clear, and
I wouldn't do so bad. We didn't sign no papers, but he
could smell it, and after two more talks he agreed to do a
dry run on three races. The first one he worked on, his
answer was the favorite, a horse named White Water, and
it won, but what the hell, it was just exercise for that rabbit.
The next one, there were two sweethearts in a field of nine,
and it was heads or tails between those two, and Heller had
the winner all right, a horse named Short Order, but on a
fifty-fifty call you don't exactly panic. But get this next
one."

Busch gestured dramatically for emphasis. "Now get it.
This animal was forty to one, but it might as well have been
four hundred. It was a musclebound sore-jointed hyena
named Zero. That alone, a horse named Zero, was enough
to put the curse of six saints on it, but also it was the kind
of looking horse which if you looked at it would make you
think promptly of canned dog food. When Heller came up
with that horse, I thought oh-oh, he's a loon after all, and
watch me run. Well, you ast me to tell you the words we
used, me and Heller. If I told you some I used when that
Zero horse won that race, you would lock me up. Not only
was Heller batting a thousand, but he had kicked through
with the most— What are you doing, taking a nap?"

We all looked at Wolfe. He was leaning back with his
eyes shut tight, and was motionless except for his lips,
which were pushing out and in, and out and in, and again
out and in. Cramer and Stebbins and I knew what that
meant: something had hit his hook, and he had yanked
and had a fish on. A tingle ran up my spine. Stebbins arose
and took a step to stand at Busch's elbow. Cramer tried
to look cynical but couldn't make it; he was as excited as
I was. The proof of it was that he didn't open his trap; he
just sat with his eyes on Wolfe, along with the rest of us,
looking at the lip movements as if they were something
really special.

"What the hell!" Busch protested. "Is he having a fit?"

Wolfe's eyes opened, and he came forward in his chair.

"No, I'm not," he snapped, "but I've been having one all evening. Mr. Cramer. Will you please have Mr. Busch removed? Temporarily."

Cramer, with no hesitation, nodded at Purley, and Purley touched Busch's shoulder, and they went. The door closed behind them, but it wasn't more than five seconds before it opened again and Purley was back with us. He wanted as quick a look at the fish as his boss and me.

"Have you ever," Wolfe was asking Cramer, "called me, pointblank, a dolt and a dotard?"

"Those aren't my words, but I've certainly called you."

"You may do so now. Your opinion of me at its lowest was far above my present opinion of myself." He looked up at the clock, which said five past three. "We now need a proper setting. How many of your staff are in my house?"

"Fourteen or fifteen."

"We want them all in here, for the effect of their presence. Half of them should bring chairs. Also, of course, the six persons we have interviewed. This shouldn't take too long—possibly an hour, though I doubt it. I certainly won't prolong it."

Cramer was looking contrary. "You've already prolonged it plenty. You mean you're prepared to name him?"

"I am not. I haven't the slightest notion who it is. But I am prepared to make an attack that will expose him—or her—and if it doesn't, I'll have no opinion of myself at all." Wolfe flattened his palms on his desk, for him a violent gesture. "Confound it, don't you know me well enough to realize when I'm ready to strike?"

"I know you too damn well." Cramer looked at his sergeant, drew in a deep breath, and let it out. "Oh, nuts. Okay, Purley. Collect the audience."

7

The office is a good-sized room, but there wasn't much unoccupied space left when that gathering was fully assembled. There were twenty-seven of us all told. The biggest assortment of Homicide employees I had ever gazed upon extended from wall to wall in the rear of the six subjects, with four of them filling the couch. Cramer was planted in the red leather chair, with Stebbins on his left, and the stenographer was hanging on at the end of my desk.

The six citizens were in a row up front, and none of them looked merry. Agatha Abbey was the only person present who rated two chairs, one for herself and one for her mink, but no one was bothering to resent it in spite of the crowding. Their minds were on other matters.

Wolfe's eyes went from right to left and back again, taking them in. He spoke. "I'll have to make this somewhat elaborate, so that all of you will clearly understand the situation. I could not at the moment hazard even a venturesome guess as to which of you killed Leo Heller, but I now know how to find out, and I propose to do so."

The only reaction visible or audible was John R. Winslow clearing his throat.

Wolfe interlaced his fingers in front of his middle mound. "We have from the first had a hint that has not been imparted to you. Yesterday—Tuesday, that is—Heller telephoned here to say that he suspected that one of his clients had committed a serious crime and to hire me to investigate. I declined, for reasons we needn't go into, but Mr. Goodwin, who is subordinate only when it suits his temperament and convenience, took it upon himself to call on Heller this morning to discuss the matter."

He shot me a glance, and I met it. Merely an incivility. He went on to them, "He entered Heller's office but found it unoccupied. Tarrying there for some minutes, and meanwhile exercising his highly trained talent for observation, he noticed, among other details, that some pencils and an eraser from an overturned jar were arranged on the desk in a sort of pattern. Later that same detail was of course noted by the police, after Heller's body had been found and they had been summoned; and it was a feature of that detail which led Mr. Cramer to come to see me. He assumed that Heller, seated at his desk and threatened with a gun, knowing or thinking he was about to die, had made the pencil pattern to leave a message, and that the purpose of the message was to give a clue to the identity of the murderer. On that point I agreed with Mr. Cramer. Will you all approach, please, and look at this arrangement on my desk? These pencils and the eraser are placed approximately the same as those on Heller's desk, with you, not me, on Heller's side of the desk. From your side you are seeing them as Heller intended them to be seen."

The six did as requested, and they had company. Not only did most of the homicide subordinates leave their chairs and come forward for a view, but Cramer himself got up and took a glance—maybe just curiosity, but I wouldn't put it past him to suspect Wolfe of a shenanigan. However, the pencils and eraser were properly placed, as I ascertained by arising and stretching to peer over shoulders.

When they were all seated again Wolfe resumed. "Mr. Cramer had a notion about the message which I rejected and will not bother to expound. My own notion of it, conceived almost immediately, came not as a coup d'éclat, but merely a stirring of memory. It reminded me vaguely of something I had seen somewhere; and the vagueness disappeared when I reflected that Heller had been a mathematician, academically qualified and trained. The memory was old, and I checked it by going to my shelves for a book I had read some ten years ago. Its title is Mathematics for the Million, by Hogben. After verifying my recollection, I locked the book in a drawer because I thought it would be a pity for Mr. Cramer to waste time leafing through it."

"Let's get on," Cramer growled.

Wolfe did so. "As told in Mr. Hogben's book, more than two thousand years ago what he calls a matchstick number script was being used in India. Three horizontal lines stood for three, two horizontal lines stood for two, and so on. That was indeed primitive, but it had greater possibilities than the clumsy devices of the Hebrews and Greeks and Romans. Around the time of the birth of Christ some brilliant Hindu improved upon it by connecting the horizontal lines with diagonals, making the units unmistakable." He pointed to the arrangement on his desk. "These five pencils on your left form a three exactly as the Hindus formed a three, and the three pencils on your right form a two. These Hindu symbols are one of the great landmarks in the history of number language. You will note, by the way, that our own forms of the figure three and of the figure two are taken directly from these Hindu symbols."

A couple of them got up to look, and Wolfe politely waited until they were seated again. "So, since Heller had been a mathematician, and since those were famous patterns in the history of mathematics, I assumed that the message was a three and a two. But evidence indicated that the eraser was also a part of the message and must be included. That was simple. It is the custom of an academic mathematician, if he wants to scribble 'four times six,' or 'seven times nine,' to use for the 'times' not an X, as we laymen do, but a dot. It is so well-known a custom that Mr. Hogben uses it in his book without thinking it necessary to explain it, and therefore I confidently assumed that the eraser was meant for a dot, and that the message was three times two, or six."

Wolfe compressed his lips and shook his head. "That was an impetuous imbecility. During the whole seven hours that I sat here poking at you people, I was trying to find some connection with the figure six that would either set one of you clearly apart, or relate you to the commission of some crime, or both. Preferably both, of course, but either would serve. In the interviews the figure six did turn up with persistent monotony, but with no promising application, and I could only ascribe it to the mischief of coincidence.

"So at three o'clock in the morning I was precisely where I had been when I started. Without a fortuitous nudge, I can't say how long it would have taken me to become aware of my egregious blunder; but I got the nudge, and I can at least say that I responded promptly and effectively. The nudge came from Mr. Busch when he mentioned the name of a horse, Zero."

He upturned a palm. "Of course. Zero! I had been a witless ass. The use of the dot as a symbol for 'times' is a strictly modern device. Since the rest of the message, the figures three and two, were in Hindu number script, surely the dot was too—provided that the Hindus had made any use of the dot. And what made my blunder so unforgivable was that the Hindus had indeed used a dot; they had used it, as is explained in Hogben's book, for the most brilliant and imaginative invention in the whole history of the language of numbers. For when you have once decided how to write three and how to write two, how are you going to distinguish among thirty-two and three hundred and two and three thousand and two and thirty thousand and two?

That was the crucial problem in number language, and the Greeks and Romans, for all their intellectual eminence, never succeeded in solving it. Some Hindu genius did, twenty centuries ago. He saw that the secret was position. Today we use our zero exactly as he did, to show position, but instead of a zero he used a dot. That's what the dot was in the early Hindu number language; it was used like our zero. So Heller's message was not three times two, or six; it was three zero two, or three hundred and two."

Susan Maturo started, jerking her head up, and made a noise. Wolfe rested his eyes on her. "Yes, Miss Maturo. Three hundred and two people died in the explosion and fire at the Montrose Hospital a month ago. You mentioned that figure when you were talking with me, but even if you hadn't, it is so imbedded in the consciousness of everyone who reads newspapers or listens to radio, it wouldn't have escaped me. The moment I realized that Heller's message was the figure three hundred and two, I would certainly have connected it with that disaster, whether you had mentioned it or not."

"But it's—" She was staring. "You mean it is connected?"

"I'm proceeding on that obvious assumption. I am assuming that through the information one of you six people furnished Leo Heller as factors for a formula, he formed a suspicion that one of you had commited a serious crime, and that his message, the figure three hundred and two, indicates that the crime was planting in the Montrose Hospital that bomb that caused the deaths of three hundred and two people—or at least involvement in that crime."

It seemed as if I could see or feel muscles tightening all over the room. Most of those dicks, maybe all of them, had of course been working on the Montrose thing. Cramer pulled his feet back and his hands were fists. Purley Stebbins took his gun from his holster and rested it on his knee and leaned forward, the better to have his eyes on all six of them.

"So," Wolfe continued, "Heller's message identified not the person who was about to kill him, not the criminal, but the crime. That was superbly ingenious, and, considering the situation he was in, he deserves our deepest admiration. He has mine, and I retract any derogation of him. It would seem natural to concentrate on Miss Maturo, since she was certainly connected with that disaster, but first let's clarify the matter. I'm going to ask the rest of you if you have at any time visited the Montrose Hospital, or been connected with it in any way, or had dealings with any of its personnel. Take the question just as I have stated it." His eyes went to the end of the row, at the left. "Mrs. Tillotson? Answer, please. Have you?"

"No." It was barely audible.

"Louder, please."

"No!"

His eyes moved. "Mr. Ennis?"

"I have not. Never."

"We'll skip you, Miss Maturo. Mr. Busch?"

"I've never been in a hospital."

"That answers only a third of the question. Answer all of it."

"The answer is no, mister."

"Miss Abbey?"

"I went there once about two years ago, to visit a patient, a friend. That was all." The tip of her tongue came out and went in. "Except for that one visit I have never been connected with it in any way or dealt with any of its personnel."

"That is explicit. Mr. Winslow?"

"No to the whole question. An unqualified no."

"Well." Wolfe did not look frustrated. "That would seem to isolate Miss Maturo, but it is not conclusive." His head turned. "Mr. Cramer. If the person who not only killed Leo Heller but also bombed that hospital is among these six, I'm sure you won't want to take the slightest risk of losing him. I have a suggestion."

"I'm listening," Cramer growled.

"Take them in as material witnesses, and hold them without bail if possible. Starting immediately, collect as many as you can of the former staff of that hospital. There were scores who survived, and other scores who were not on duty at the time. Get all of them if possible, spare no effort, and have them look at these people and say if they have ever seen any of them. Meanwhile, of course, you will be working on Miss Maturo, but you have heard the denials of the other five, and if you get reliable evidence that one of them has lied I'm sure you will need no further suggestion from me. Indeed, if one of them has lied and leaves this room in custody with that lie undeclared, that alone will be half the battle. I'm sorry—"

"Wait a minute."

All eyes went to one spot. It was Jack Ennis, the inventor. His thin colorless lips were twisted, with one end up, but not in an attempt to smile. The look in his eyes showed that he had no idea of smiling.

"I didn't tell an exact lie," he said.

Wolfe's eyes were slits. "Then an inexact lie, Mr. Ennis?"

"I mean I didn't visit that hospital as a hospital. And I didn't have dealings with them, I was just trying to. I wanted them to give my X-ray machine a trial. One of them was willing to, but the other two talked him down."

"When was this?"

"I was there three times, twice in December and once in January."

"I thought your X-ray machine had a flaw."

"It wasn't perfect, but it would work, and it would have been better than anything they had. I was sure I was going to get it in, because he was for it—his name is Halsey—and I saw him first, and he wanted to try it. But the other two talked him out of it, and one of them was very—he—" He petered out.

Wolfe prodded him. "Very what, Mr. Ennis?"

"He didn't understand me! He hated me!"

"There are people like that. There are all kinds of people. Have you ever invented a bomb?"

"A bomb?" Ennis's lips worked, and this time I thought he actually was trying to smile. "Why would I invent a bomb?"

"I don't know. Inventors invent many things. If you have never tried your hand at a bomb, of course you have never had occasion to get hold of the necessary materials—for instance, explosives. It's only fair to tell you what I now regard as a reasonable hypothesis: that you placed the bomb in the hospital in revenge for an injury, real or fancied; that included in the data you gave Leo Heller was an item or items which led him to suspect you of that crime; that something he said led you, in turn, to suspect that he suspected; that when you went to his place this morning you went armed, prepared for action if your suspicion was verified; that when you entered the building you recognized Mr. Goodwin as my assistant; that you went up to Heller's office and asked him if Mr. Goodwin was there for an appointment with him, and his answer heightened or confirmed your suspicion, and you produced the gun; that—"

"Hold it," Cramer snapped. "I'll take it from here. Purley, get him out and—"

Purley was a little slow. He was up, but Ennis was up faster and off in a flying dive for Wolfe. I dived too, and got an arm and jerked. He tore loose, but by then a whole squad was there, swarming into him, and since I wasn't needed I backed off. As I did so someone dived at me, and Susan Maturo was up against me, gripping my lapels.

"Tell me!" she demanded. "Tell me! Was it him?"

I told her promptly and positively, to keep her from ripping my lapels off. "Yes," I said, in one word.

Two months later a jury of eight men and four women agreed with me.

This Won't Kill You

1

At the end of the sixth inning the score was Boston 11, New York 1.

I would not have believed that the day would ever come when, seated in a lower box between home and first, at the seventh and deciding game of the World Series between the Giants and Red Sox, I would find myself glomming a girl, no matter who. I am by no means above glomming a girl if she is worthy, but not at the Polo Grounds, where my mind is otherwise occupied. That awful day, though, I did.

The situation was complex and will have to be explained. It was a mess even before the game started. Pierre Mondor, owner of the famous Mondor's Restaurant in Paris, was visiting New York and was our house guest. He got the notion, God knows how or why, that Wolfe had to take him to a baseball game, and Wolfe's conception of the obligations of a host wouldn't let him use his power of veto. Tickets were no problem, since Emil Chisholm, oil millionaire and part-owner of the Giants, considered himself deeply in Wolfe's debt on account of a case we had handled for him a few years back.

So that October afternoon, a Wednesday, I got the pair

of them, the noted private detective and the noted chef, up to the Polo Grounds in a taxi, steered them through the mob into the entrance, along the concrete ramps, and down the aisle to our box. It was twenty past one—only ten minutes to game time—and the stands were jammed. I motioned to Mondor, and he slid in and sat. Wolfe stood and glared down at the wooden slats and metal arms. Then he lifted his head and glared at me.

"Are you out of your senses?" he demanded.

"I warned you," I said coldly. "It was designed for men, not mammoths. Let's go home."

He tightened his lips, moved his massivity, lowered it, and tried to squeeze between the arms. No. He grasped the rail in front with both hands, wriggled loose, and got what he could of his fanny hooked on the edge of the seat.

Mondor called to me across the great expanse of Wolfe's back, "I depend with confidence on you, Arshee! You must make clear as it develops! What are the little white things?"

I love baseball and I love the Giants, and I had fifty bucks up on that game, but I would have got up and gone but for one thing. It was working hours, and Wolfe pays my salary, and there were too many people, some of them alive and loose, who felt strongly that he had already lived too long. He is seldom out in the open, easy to get at, and when he is I like to be nearby. So I gritted my teeth and stuck.

The ground crew finished smoothing off and hauled their drags away, the umpires did a huddle, the Giants trotted out on the field to their stations, the throng gave with a lusty excited roar, we all stood up for "The Star-Spangled Banner" and then sat again, with Wolfe perched on two slats and holding grimly to the rail. After southpaw Ed Romeike, 22-4 for the season, had burned a few over for the range, Lew Baker, the catcher, fired it to Tiny Garth at second. The Red Sox lead-off man came to the white line, the plate umpire said go, and Romeike looked around at the field, toed the rubber, went into his tricky windup, and shot a fast one over the outside corner for strike one. The crowd let out a short sharp yell.

My personal nightmare was bad enough. Mondor was our guest, and only eighteen hours ago I had taken three helpings of the quenelles bonne femme he had cooked in our kitchen, and would have made it four if I had had room; but trying to tell a foreigner what a base on balls is during a World Series game, with two men on, two down, and Oaky Asmussen at bat, is hard on the nerves. As for Wolfe, it wasn't so much the sight of him there in his concentrated misery; it was the certainty that by tomorrow he would have figured out a way to blame it on me, and that would start a feud.

Bad enough, but more was to come, and not for me alone. One fly had plopped into the soup even before the game started, when the line-up was announced and Tiny Garth was named for second base, with no explanation. A buzz of amazement had filled the stands. Why not Nick Ferrone? Ferrone, a lanky big-eared kid just up from the bush five months back, had fielded and batted himself so far to the front that it was taken for granted he would be voted rookie of the year. He had been spectacular in the first six games of the series, batting .427. Where was he today? Why Garth?

Then the game. This was no personal nightmare of mine, it was all too public. In the first inning Con Prentiss, the Giants' shortstop, bobbled an easy grounder, and two minutes later Lew Baker, the catcher, trying to nab a runner at second, threw the ball six feet over Garth's head into the outfield. With luck, the Red Sox scored only one run. In the second inning Nat Neill, center fielder, misjudged a fly he could have walked under, tried to run in three directions at once, and had to chase it to the fence; and soon after that Prentiss grabbed a hard-hit ball on the hop and hurled it into the dirt three paces to the left of third base. By the time they got three out, Boston had two more runs.

As the Giants came in for their turn at bat in the second, heading for the dugout, loud and bitter sarcasms from the stands greeted them. Then our section was distracted by an incident. A man in a hurry came plunging down the aisle, bumping my elbow as he passed, and pulled up alongside a front box occupied by six men, among them the Mayor of New York and oilman Emil Chisholm, who had provided our tickets. The man spoke into the ear of Chisholm, who looked anything but happy. Chisholm said something to the Mayor and to another of his boxmates, arose and sidled out, and beat it up the aisle double quick, followed by the courier and also by cutting remarks from nearby fans who had recognized him. As my eyes went back to the arena, Con Prentiss, the Giant shortstop, swung at a floater and missed by a mile.

There is no point in my retailing the agony. As I said, at the end of the sixth the score was 11 to 1. Romeike was doing all right, and Boston had collected only three hits, but his support would have been pitiful on a sandlot. Joe Eston and Nat Neill had each made two errors, and Con Prentiss and Lew Baker three apiece. As they came to the dugout in the sixth, one wit yelled, "Say it ain't so, Joe!" at Eston, and the crowd, recognizing that classic moan to Shoeless Joe Jackson, let out a howl. They were getting really rough. As for me, I had had plenty of the tragedy out on the diamond and looked around for something less painful, and caught sight of the girl, in a box off to my right.

I glommed her, not offensively. Ther were two of them. One was a redhead who would start to get plump in a couple of years, almost worthy, but not quite. The other one, the glommee, had light brown hair and dark brown eyes, and was fully qualified. I had the feeling that she was not a complete stranger, that I had seen her some-where before, but couldn't place her. The pleasure it gave me to look at her was not pure, because it was adulterated with resentment. She looked happy. Her eyes sparkled. Apparently she liked the way things were going. There is no law barring Boston fans from the Polo Grounds, but I resented it. Nevertheless, I continued the glommation. She was the only object I had seen there that day, on or off the field, that didn't make me want to shut my eyes and keep them shut, and I sure needed it.

Something came between her and me. A man stopped at my elbow, leaned down, and asked my ear, "Are you Archie Goodwin?"

I told him yes.

"Is that Nero Wolfe?"

I nodded.

"Mr. Chisholm wants him in the clubhouse, quick."

I reflected for two seconds, decided that this was straight

from heaven, and slid forward to tell Wolfe, "Mr. Chisholm invites us to the clubhouse. We'll avoid the crush. There's a chair there. He want to see you."

He didn't even growl, "What about?" He didn't even growl. Turning to mutter something to Mondor, he pulled himself erect and sidestepped past me to the aisle. Mondor came after him. The courier led the way, and I brought up the rear.

As we went up the concrete steps, single file, a shout came from somewhere on the left. "Go get 'em, Nerol Sick 'em!"

Such is fame.

2

"This is urgent!" Emil Chisholm squeaked. "It's urgent!"

There was no chair in the clubroom of the size Wolfe likes and needs, but there was a big leather couch, and he was on it, breathing hard and scowling. Mondor was seated over against the wall, out of it. Chisholm, a hefty broad-shouldered guy not as tall as me, with a wide thick mouth and a long straight nose, was too upset to stand or sit, so he was boiling around. I was standing near an open window. Through it came a sudden swelling roar from the crowd out in the stands.

"Shut that goddam window!" Chisholm barked.

I did so.

"I'm going home," Wolfe stated in his most conclusive tone. "But not until they have left. Perhaps, if you will tell me briefly—"

"We've lost the series!" Chisholm shouted.

Wolfe closed his eyes and opened them again. "If you'll keep your voice down?" he suggested. "I've had enough noise today. If losing the series is your problem, I'm afraid I can't help."

"No. Nobody can." Chisholm stood facing him. "I blew up, damn it, and I've got to get hold of myself. This is what happened. Out there before the game Art got a suspicion—"

"Art?"

"Art Kinney, our manager. Naturally he was watching

the boys like a hawk, and he got a suspicion something was wrong. That first—"

"Why was he watching them like a hawk?"

"That's his job! He's manager!" Chisholm realized he was shouting again, stopped, clamped his jaw and clenched his fists, and after a second went on. "Also Nick Ferrone had disappeared. He was here with them in the clubhouse, he had got into uniform, and after they went out and were in the dugout he just wasn't there. Art sent Doc Soffer back here to get him, but he couldn't find him. He was simply gone. Art had to put Garth at second base. Naturally he was on edge, and he noticed things, the way some of the boys looked and acted, that made him suspicious. Then—"

A door opened and a guy came running in, yelling, "Fitch hit one and Neill let it get by and Asmussen scored! Fitch went on to third!"

I recognized him, chiefly by his crooked nose, which had got in the way of a line drive back in the twenties when he was a Cardinal infielder. He was Beaky Durkin, now a Giant scout, with a recent new lease on life because he had dug up Nick Ferrone out in Arkansas.

Chisholm jerked his arms up and pushed palms at Durkin. "Get out! Get the hell out!" He took a threatening step. "Send Doc—hey, Doc! Come in here!"

Durkin, backing out, collided with another in the doorway. The other was Doc Soffer, the Giants' veteran medico, bald, wearing black-rimmed glasses, with a long torso and short legs. Entering, he looked as if his ten best-paying patients had just died on him.

"I can't sweat it, Doc," Chisholm told him. "I'm nuts. This is Nero Wolfe. You tell him."

"Who are you?" Wolfe demanded.

Soffer stood before him. "I'm Doctor Horton Soffer," he said, clipping it. "Four of my men, possible five, have been drugged. They're out there now, trying to play ball, and they can't." He stopped, looking as if he were about to break down and cry, gulped twice, and went on. "They didn't seem right, there in the dugout. I noticed it, and so did Kinney. That first inning there was no doubt about it, something was wrong. The second inning it was even worse—the same four men, Baker, Prentiss, Neill, and

Eston—and I got an idea. I told Kinney, and he sent me here to investigate. You see that cooler?"

He pointed to a big white-enameled electric refrigerator standing against a wall. Mondor, seated near it, was staring at us.

Wolfe nodded. "Well?"

"It contains mostly an assortment of drinks in bottles. I know my men's habits—every little habit they've got, and big one too. I knew that after they get into uniform before a game those four men—the four I named—have the habit of getting a bottle of Beebright out of the cooler and—"

"What is Beebright?"

"It's a carbonated drink that is supposed to have honey in it instead of sugar. Each of those four drinks a bottle of it, or part of one, before he goes out to the field, practically without exception. And it was those four that were off—terrible; I never saw anything like it. That's why I got my idea. Kinney was desperate and told me to come and see, and I did. Usually the clubhouse boy cleans up here after the men leave for the field, but this being the deciding game of the World Series, today he didn't. Stuff was scattered around—as you see, it still is—and there was a Beebright bottle there on that table with a little left in it. It didn't smell wrong, and I didn't want to waste any tasting it. I had sent for Mr. Chisholm, and when he came we decided what to do. He sent for Beaky Durkin, who had a seat in the grandstand, because he knew Ferrone better than anyone else and might have some idea that would help. I took the Beebright down the street to a drugstore, and made two tests. The first one, Ranwez's, didn't prove anything, but that was probably because it is limited—"

"Negatives may be skipped," Wolfe muttered.

"I'm telling you what I did," Soffer snapped. He was trying to keep calm. "Ranwez's test took over half an hour. The second, Ekkert's, took less. I did it twice, to check. It was conclusive. The Beebright contained sodium phenobarbital. I couldn't get the quantity, in a hurry like that, but on a guess it was two grains, possibly a little more, in the full bottle. Anyone can get hold if it. Certainly that would be no problem for a bigtime gambler who wanted to clean up on a World Series game. And—"

"The sonofabitch," Chisholm said.

Doc Soffer nodded. "And another sonofabitch put it in the bottles, knowing those four men would drink it just before the game. All he had to do was remove the caps, drop the tablets in, replace the caps, and shake the bottles a little—not much, because it's very soluble. It must have been done today after twelve o'clock, because otherwise someone else might have drunk it, and anyway, if it were done much in advance the drinks would have gone stale, and those men would have noticed it. So it must have been someone—"

Chisholm had marched to the window. He whirled and yelled, "Ferrone did it, damn him! He did it and lammed!"

Beaky Durkin appeared. He came through the door and halted, facing Chisholm. He was trembling, and his face was white, all but the crooked nose.

"Not Nick," he said hoarsely. "Not that boy. Nick didn't do it, Mr. Chisholm!"

"Oh, no?" Chisholm was bitter. "Did I ask you? A fine rookie of the year you brought in from Arkansas! Where is he? Get him and bring him in again and let me get my hands on him! Go find him! Will you go find him?"

"Go where?"

"How the hell do I know? Have you any idea where he is?"

"No."

"Will you go find him?"

Durkin lifted helpless hands and dropped them.

"He's your pet, not mine," Chisholm said savagely. "Get him and bring him in, and I'll offer him a new contract. That will be a contract. Beat it!"

Durkin left through the door he had entered by.

Wolfe grunted. "Sit down, please," he told Chisholm. "When I address you I look at you, and my neck is not elastic. Thank you, sir. You want to hire me for a job?"

"Yes. I want—"

"Please. Is this correct? Four of your best players, drugged as described by Doctor Soffer, could not perform properly, and as a result a game is lost, and a World Series?"

"We're losing it." Chisholm's head swung toward the window and back again. "Of course it's lost."

"And you assume a gambler or a group of gamblers is responsible. How much could he or they win on a game?"

"On today's game, any amount. Fifty thousand or double that, easy."

"I see. Then you need the police. At once."

Chisholm shook his head. "Damn it, I don't want to. Baseball is a wonderful game, a clean game, the best and cleanest game on earth. This is the dirtiest thing that's happened in baseball in thirty years, and it's got to be handled right and handled fast. You're the best detective in the business, and you're right here. With a swarm of cops trooping in, God knows what will happen. If we have to have them later, all right, but now here you are. Go to it!"

Wolfe was frowning. "You think this Nick Ferrone did it."

"I don't know!" Chisholm was yelling again. "How do I know what I think? He's a harebrained kid just out of the sticks, and he's disappeared. Where'd he go and why? What does that look like?"

Wolfe nodded. "Very well." He drew a deep sigh. "I can at least make some gestures and see." He aimed a finger at the door Beaky Durkin and Doc Soffer had used. "Is that an office?"

"It leads to Kinney's office—the manager."

"Then it has a phone. You will call police headquarters and report the disappearance of Nick Ferrone, and ask them to find him. Such a job, when urgent, is beyond my resources. Tell them nothing more for the present if you want it that way. Where do the players change clothing?"

"Through there." Chisholm indicated another door. "The locker room. The shower room is beyond."

Wolfe's eyes came to me. "Archie. You will look around. All contiguous premises except this room, which you can leave to me."

"Anything in particular?" I asked.

"No. You have good eyes and a head of sorts. Use them."

"I could wait to phone the police," Chisholm suggested, "until you—"

"No," Wolfe snapped. "In ten minutes you can have ten thousand men looking for Mr. Ferrone, and it will cost you ten cents. Spend it. I charge more for less."

Chisholm went, through the door at the left, with Doc Soffer at his heels. Since Wolfe had said "all contiguous premises," I thought I might as well start in that direction, and followed them, across a hall and into another room. It was good-sized, furnished with desks, chairs, and accessories. Beaky Durkin was on a chair in a corner with his ear to a radio turned low, and Doc Soffer was heading for him. Chisholm barked, "Shut that damn thing off!" and crossed to a desk with a phone. Under other circumstances I would have enjoyed having a look at the office of Art Kinney, the Giants' manager, but I was on a mission and there was too big an audience. I about-faced and back-tracked. As I crossed the clubroom to the door in the far wall, Wolfe was standing by the open door of the refrigerator with a bottle of Beebright in his hand, holding it at arm's length, sneering at it, and Mondor was beside him. I passed through, and was in a room both long and wide, with two rows of lockers, benches and stools, and a couple of chairs. The locker doors were marked with numbers and names too. I tried three; they were locked. After going through a doorway to the left, I was in the shower room. The air in there was a little damp, but not warm. I went to the far end, glancing in at each of the shower stalls, was disappointed to see no pillbox that might have contained sodium phenobarbital, and returned to the locker room.

In the middle of the row on the right was the locker marked "Ferrone." Its door was locked. With my portable key collection I could have operated, but I don't take it along to ball games, and nothing on my personal ring was usable. It seemed to me that the inside of that locker was the one place that needed attention, certainly the first on the list, so I returned to the clubroom, made a face at Wolfe as I went by, and entered Kinney's office. Chisholm had finished phoning and was seated at a desk, staring at the floor. Beaky Durkin and Doc Soffer had their ears glued to the radio, which was barely audible.

I asked Chisholm, "Have you got a key to Ferrone's locker?"

His head jerked up, and he said aggressively, "What?"

"I want a key to Ferrone's locker."

"I haven't got one. I think Kinney has a master key. I don't know where he keeps it."

"Fifteen to two," Durkin informed us, or maybe just talking to himself. "Giants batting in the ninth, two down. Garth got a home run, bases empty. It's all—"

"Shut up!" Chisholm yelled at him.

Since Kinney would soon be with us, and since Ferrone's locker had first call, I thought I might as well wait there for him. However, with our client sitting there glaring at me, it would be well to display some interest and energy, so I moved. I took in the room. I went to filing cabinets and looked them over. I opened a door, saw a hall leading to stairs down, backed up, and shut the door. I took in the room again, crossed to another door in the opposite wall, and opened that.

Since I hadn't the faintest expectation of finding anything pertinent beyond that door, let alone a corpse, I must have made some sound or movement in my surprise, but if so it wasn't noticed. I stood for three seconds, then slipped inside and squatted long enough to get an answer to the main question.

I arose, backed out, and addressed Soffer. "Take a look here, Doc. I think he's dead. If so, watch it."

He made a noise, stared, and moved. I marched out, into the clubroom, crossed to Wolfe, and spoke. "Found something. I opened a door to a closet and found Nick Ferrone, in uniform, on the floor, with a baseball bat alongside him and his head smashed in. He's dead, according to me, but Doc Soffer is checking, if you want an expert opinion. Found on contiguous premises."

Wolfe grunted. He was seated on the leather couch. "Mr. Ferrone?" he asked peevishly.

"Yes, sir."

"You found him?"

"Yes, sir."

His shoulders went up a quarter of an inch and down again. "Call the police."

"Yes, sir. A question. Any minute the ballplayers will be coming in here. The cops won't like it if they mess around. The cops will think we should have prevented it. Do we care? It probably won't be Cramer. Do we—"

A bellow, Chisholm's, came through. "Wolfe! Come in here! Come here!"

He got up, growling. "We owe the police nothing, certainly not deference. But we have a client—I think we have. I'll see. Meanwhile you stay here. Everyone entering this room remains, under surveillance." He headed for Kinney's office, whence more bellows were coming.

Another door opened, the one in the west wall, and Nat Neill, the Giants' center fielder, entered, his jaw set and his eyes blazing. Following him came Lew Baker, the catcher. Behind them, on the stairs, was a clatter of footsteps.

The game was over. The Giants had lost.

3

Another thing I don't take along to ball games is a gun, but that day there was a moment when I wished I had. After any ordinary game, even a lost one, I suppose the Giants might have been merely irritated if, on getting to the clubhouse, they found a stranger there, backed up against the door to the locker room, who told them firmly that on account of a state of emergency they could not pass. But that day they were ready to plug one another, so why not a stranger?

The first dozen were ganging me, about to start using hands, when Art Kinney, the manager, appeared, strode across, and wanted to know what. I told him to go to his office and ask Chisholm. The gang let up then, to consider —all but Bill Moyse, the second-string catcher, six feet two, and over two hundred pounds. He had come late, after Kinney. He breasted up to me, making fists, and announced that his wife was waiting for him and he was going in to change, and either I would move or he would move me. One of his teammates called from the rear, "Show him her picture, Bill! That'll move him!"

Moyse whirled and leaped. Hands grabbed for him, but he kept going. Whether he reached his target and actually landed or not I can't say, because, first, I was staying put and it was quite a mixup, and second, I was seeing something that wasn't present. The mention of Moyse's wife and her picture had done it. What I was seeing was a picture of a girl that had appeared in the *Gazette* a couple of months back, with a caption tagging her as the showgirl bride of William Moyse, the ballplayer; and it was the girl I had been glomming in a nearby box when the summons had come from Chisholm. No question about it. That was interesting, and possibly even relevant.

Meanwhile Moyse was doing me a service by making a diversion. Three or four had hold of him, and others were gathered around his target, Con Prentiss, the shortstop. They were all jabbering. Prentiss, who was wiry and tough, was showing his teeth in a grin—not an attractive one. Moyse suddenly whirled again and was back at me, and this time, obviously, he was coming through. It was useless to start slugging that mountain of muscle, and I was set to try locking him, hoping the others would admire the performance, when a loud voice came from the doorway to the manager's office.

"Here! Attention, all of you!"

It was Art Kinney. His face was absolutely white, and his neck cords were twitching, as they all turned and were silent.

"I'm full up," he said, half hysterical. "This is Nero Wolfe, the detective. He'll tell you something."

Muttering went around as Kinney stepped aside and Wolfe took his place in the doorway. Wolfe's eyes darted from left to right, and he spoke.

"You deserve an explanation, gentlemen, but the police are coming and there's not much time. You have just lost a ball game by knavery. Four of you were drugged, in a drink called Beebright, and could not perform properly. You will learn—"

They drowned him out. It was an explosion of astonished rage.

"Gentlemen!" Wolfe thundered. "Will you listen?" He glowered. "You will learn more of that later, but there is something more urgent. The dead body of one of your colleagues, Mr. Nick Ferrone, has been discovered on these premises. He was murdered. It is supposed, naturally, that the two events, the drugging and the murder, are connected. In any case, if you do not know what a murder investigation means to everyone within reach, innocent or not, you are about to learn. For the moment you will not leave this room. When the police arrive they will tell you—"

Heavy feet were clomping in the hall. A door swung open, and a uniformed cop stepped in, followed by three others. The one in front, a sergeant, halted and demanded indignantly, "What is all this? Where is it?"

The Giants looked at the cops and hadn't a word to say.

4

Inspector Hennessy of uptown Homicide was tall and straight, silver-haired, with a bony face and quick-moving gray eyes. Some two years ago he had told Nero Wolfe that if he ever again tried poking into a murder in his territory he would be escorted to the Harlem River and dunked. But when, at nine o'clock that evening, Hennessy breezed through the clubroom, passing in front of the leather couch where Wolfe was seated with a ham sandwich in one hand and a bottle of beer in the other, he didn't even toss a glance. He was much too busy.

The police commissioner was in Manager Kinney's office with Chisholm and others. The district attorney and an assistant were in the locker room, along with an assortment of Homicide men, giving various athletes their third or fourth quiz. There were still a couple of dozen city employees in the clubhouse, though the scientists—the photographers and fingerprint hounds—had all finished and gone.

I had standing as the finder of the corpse, but also I was a part of Wolfe. Technically Wolfe was not poking into a murder; he had been hired by Chisholm, before the corpse had been found, to find out who had doped the ballplayers. However, in gathering facts for relay to Wolfe, I had not discriminated. I saw Nick Ferrone's locker opened and the contents examined, with nothing startling disclosed. While I was in Kinney's office watching a basket squad load the corpse and carry it out, I heard a lieutenant on the phone giving instructions for a roundup of gamblers throughout the metropolitan area. A little later I picked up a bunch of signed statements from a table and sat down and read them through, without anyone's noticing. By that time the commissioner and the DA had arrived, and they had eight or nine quiz posts going in the various rooms, and Hennessy was doing his damnedest to keep it organized.

I collected all I could for Wolfe. The bat that had been used to crack Ferrone's skull was no stock item, but a valued trophy. With it, years back, a famous Giant had belted a grand slam home run that had won a pennant, and the bat had been displayed on a wall rack in the manager's office. The murderer could have simply grabbed it from the rack. It had no usable fingerprints. Of eight bottles of Beebright left in the cooler, the two in front had been doped, and the other six had not. No other drinks had been tampered with. Everyone had known of the liking of those four—Baker, Prentiss, Neill, and Eston—for Beebright, and their habit of drinking a bottle of it before a game. No good prints. No sign anywhere of any container of tablets of sodium phenobarbital. And a thousand other negatives—for instance, the clubhouse boy, Jimmie Burr. The custom was that, when he wasn't around, the players would put chits in a little box for what they took, and he hadn't been around. For that game someone had got him a box seat, and he had beat it to the grandstand while most of the players were in the locker room changing. A sergeant jumped on it: who had got him out of the way by providing a ticket for a box seat? But it had been Art Kinney himself, the manager.

Around eight o'clock they turned a big batch loose. Twenty Giants, including coaches and the bat boy, were allowed to go to the locker room to change, under surveillance, and then let out, with instructions to keep available. They were not in the picture as it then looked. It was established that Ferrone had arrived at the clubhouse shortly after twelve o'clock and had got into uniform; a dozen of them had been in the locker room when he had. He had been present during a pre-game session with Kinney in the clubroom, and no one remembered seeing him leave afterward. After they had trooped out and down the stairs, emerged onto the field, and crossed it, Ferrone's absence was not noticed until they had been in the dugout some minutes. As the cops figured it, he couldn't have been slammed with a baseball bat in Kinney's office, only a few yards away, while the team was in the clubroom, and therefore all who had unquestionably left for the field with the gang, and had stayed there, were in the clear until further notice. With them went Pierre Mondor, who had wanted to see a ball game and had picked a beaut.

As I said, when Inspector Hennessy breezed through the clubroom at nine o'clock, coming from the locker room and headed for Kinney's office, he didn't even toss a glance at the leather couch where Wolfe and I were seated. He disappeared. But soon he was back again, speaking from the doorway.

"Come in here, will you, Wolfe?"

"No," Wolfe said flatly. "I'm eating."

"The commissioner wants you."

"Is he eating?" Waiting for no reply, Wolfe turned his head and bellowed, "Mr. Skinner! I'm dining!"

It wasn't very polite, I thought, to be sarcastic about the sandwiches and beer Chisholm had provided. Hennessy started a remark which indicated that he agreed with me, but it was interrupted by the appearance of Commissioner Skinner at his elbow. Hennessy stepped in and aside, and Skinner entered, followed by Chisholm, and approached the couch. He spoke. "Dining?"

"Yes, sir." Wolfe reached for another sandwich. "As you see."

"Not your accustomed style."

Wolfe grunted and bit into the sandwich.

Skinner kept it friendly. "I've just learned that four men who were told they could go are still here—Baker, Prentiss, Neill, and Eston. When Inspector Hennessy asked them why, they told him that Mr. Chisholm asked them to stay. Mr. Chisholm says that he did so at your suggestion. He understood that you want to speak with them after our men have all left. Is that correct?"

Wolfe nodded. "I made it quite plain, I thought."

"M-m-m-m." The commissioner regarded him. "You see, I know you fairly well. You wouldn't dream of hanging on here half the night to speak with those men merely as a routine step in an investigation. And besides, at Mr. Chisholm's request you have already been permitted to speak with them, and with several others. You're cooking something. Those are the four men who were drugged, but they left the clubhouse for the field with the rest of the team, so, the way we figure it, none of them killed Ferrone. How do you figure it?"

Wolfe swallowed the last of a well-chewed bite. "I don't."

Hennessy growled and set his jaw. Skinner said, "I don't believe it," with his tone friendlier than his words. "You're cooking something," he insisted. "What's the play with those four men?"

Wolfe shook his head. "No, sir."

Hennessy took a step forward. "Look," he said, "this is my territory. My name's Hennessy. You don't turn *this* murder into a parlor game."

Wolfe raised brows at him. "Murder? I am not concerned with murder. Mr. Chisholm hired me to investigate the drugging of his employees. The two events may of course be connected, but the murder is your job. And they were not necessarily connected. I understand that a man named Moyse is in there now with the district attorney"
—Wolfe aimed a thumb at the door to the locker room—
"because it has been learned that he has twice within a month assaulted Mr. Ferrone physically, through resentment at Ferrone's interest in his wife, injudiciously displayed. And that Moyse did not leave the clubhouse with the others, and arrived at the dugout three or four minutes later, just before Ferrone's absence was noticed. For your murder, Mr. Hennessy, that should be a help; but it doesn't get me on with my job, disclosure of the culprit who drugged the drinks. Have you charged Mr. Moyse?"

"No." Hennessy was curt. "So you're not interested in the murder?"

"Not as a job, since it's not mine. But if you want a comment from a specialist, you're closing your lines too soon."

"We haven't closed any lines."

"You let twenty men walk out of here. You are keeping Moyse for the reasons given. You are keeping Doctor Soffer, I suppose, because when Ferrone was missed in the dugout Soffer came here to look for him, and he could have found him here alive and killed him. You are keeping Mr. Durkin, I suppose again, because he too could have been here alone with Ferrone. He says he left the clubhouse shortly before the team did and went to his seat in the grandstand, and stayed there. Has he been either contradicted or corroborated?"

"No."

"Then you regard him as vulnerable on opportunity?"

"Yes."

"Are you holding Mr. Chisholm for the same reason?"

Chisholm made a noise. Skinner and Hennessy stared. Skinner said, "We're not holding Mr. Chisholm."

"You should be, for consistency," Wolfe declared. "This afternoon, when I reached my seat in the stands—of which only the front edge was accessible to me—at twenty minutes past one, the Mayor and others were there in a nearby box, but Mr. Chisholm was not. He arrived a few minutes later. He has told me that when he arrived with his party, including the Mayor, about one o'clock, he had the others escorted to the stands and the box, that he started for the clubhouse for a word with his employees, that he was delayed by the crowd and decided it was too late, that he went on a private errand to a men's room and then proceeded to the box. If the others are vulnerable on opportunity, so is he."

They made remarks, all three of them, not appreciative. Wolfe put the bottle to his lips, tilted it and his head, and swallowed beer. Paper cups had been supplied, but he hates them.

He put the bottle down empty. "I was merely," he said mildly, "commenting on the murder as a specialist. As for my job, learning who drugged the drinks, I haven't even made a start. How could I in this confounded hubbub? Trampled by an army. I have been permitted to sit here and talk to people, yes, with a succession of your subordinates standing behind me, breathing down my neck. One of them was chewing gum! Pfui. Working on a murder and chewing gum!"

"We'll bounce him," Hennessy said dryly. "The commissioner has asked you, what's the play with those four men?"

Wolfe shook his head. "Not only those four. I included others in my request to Mr. Chisholm—Doctor Soffer, Mr. Kinney, Mr. Durkin, and of course Mr. Chisholm himself. I am not arranging a parlor game. I make a living as a professional detective, and I need their help on this job

I've undertaken. I think I know why, engrossed as you are with the most sensational case you've had in years, you're spending all this time chatting with me; you suspect I'm contriving a finesse. Don't you?"

"You're damn right we do."

Wolfe nodded. "So I am."

"You are?"

"Yes." Wolfe suddenly was peevish. "Haven't I sat here for five hours, submerged in your pandemonium? Haven't you all the facts that I have, and many more besides? Haven't you a thousand men to command—indeed, twenty thousand—and I one? One little fact strikes me as apparently it has not struck you, and in my forlorn desperation I decided to test my interpretation of it. For that test I need help, and I ask Mr. Chisholm to provide it, and—"

"We'll be glad to help," Skinner cut in. "Which fact, and how do you interpret it?"

"No, sir." Wolfe was positive. "It is my one slender chance to earn a fee. I intend—"

"We may not know this fact."

"Certainly you do. I have stated it explicitly during this conversation, but I won't point at it for you. If I did you'd spoil it for me, and, slender as it is, I intend to test it. I am not beset with the urgency of murder, as you are, but I'm in a fix. I don't need a motive strong enough to incite a man to murder, merely one to persuade him to drug some bottled drinks—mildly, far from lethally. A thousand dollars? Twenty thousand? That would be only a fraction of the possible winnings on a World Series game—and no tax to pay. The requisitions of the income tax have added greatly to the attractions of mercenary crime. As for opportunity, anyone at all could have slipped in here late this morning, before others had arrived, with drugged bottles of that drink and put them in the cooler—and earned a fortune. Those twenty men you let go, Mr. Hennessy—of how many of them can you say positively that they did not drug the drinks?"

The inspector was scowling at him. "I can say that I don't think any of them killed Ferrone."

"Ah, but I'm not after the murderer; that's your job." Wolfe upturned a palm. "You see why I am driven to a forlorn finesse. It is my only hope of avoiding a laborious and possibly fruitless—"

What interrupted him was the entry of a man through the door to the locker room. District Attorney Megalech was as masterful as they come, although bald as a doorknob. He strode across and told Skinner and Hennessy he wanted to speak with them, took an elbow of each, and steered them to and through the door to Kinney's office. Chisholm, uninvited, wheeled and followed them.

Wolfe reached for a sandwich and took a healthy bite. I arose, brushed off crumbs, shook my pants legs down, and stood looking down at him. I asked, "How good is this fact you're saving up?"

"Not very." He chewed and swallowed. "Good enough to try if we got nothing better. Evidently they have nothing at all. If they had—but you heard them."

"Yeah. You told them they have all the facts you have, but they haven't. The one I gave you about Mrs. Moyse? That's not the one you're interpreting privately?"

"No."

"She might be still around, waiting. I might possibly get something better than the one you're saving. Shall I go try?"

He grunted. I took it for a yes, and moved. Outside the door to the hall and stairs stood one in uniform with whom I had already had a few little words. I addressed him. "I'm going down to buy Mr. Wolfe a pickle. Do I need to be passed out or in?"

"You?" He used only the right half of his mouth for talking. "Shoot your way through. Huh?"

"Right. Many thanks." I went.

5

It was dumb to be so surprised, but I was. I might have known that the news that the Giants had been doped out of the game and the series, and that Nick Ferrone, the probable rookie of the year, had been murdered, would draw a record mob. Downstairs inside the entrance there were sentries, and outside a regiment was stretched into a cordon. I was explaining to a sergeant who I was and telling him I would be returning, when three desperate men, one of whom I recognized, came springing at me. All they wanted was the truth, the whole truth, and nothing but the truth. I had to get really rude. I have been clawed at by newspapermen more than once, but I had never seen them quite as hungry as they were outside the Polo Grounds that October night. Finding they wouldn't shake loose, I dived through the cordon and into the mob.

It looked hopeless. The only parked cars in sight on the west side of Eighth Avenue were police cars. I pushed through to the fringe of the throng and made my way two blocks south. Having made inquiries of two Giants hours previously, I knew what I was looking for, a light blue Curtis sedan. Of course there was a thin chance that it was still around, but if it was I wanted it. I crossed the avenue and headed for the parking plaza. Two cops at the end of the cordon gave me a look, but it wasn't the plaza they were guarding, and I marched on through. In the dim light I could see three cars over at the north end. Closer up, one was a Curtis sedan. Still closer, it was light blue. I went up to it. Two females on the front seat were gazing at me through the window, and one of them was my glommee. The radio was on. I opened the door, swung it wide, and said hello.

"Who are you?" she demanded.

"My name's Archie Goodwin. I'll show credentials if you are Mrs. William Moyse."

"What do you want?"

"Nothing if you're not Mrs. Moyse."

"What if I am?"

She was rapidly erasing the pleasant memory I had of her. Not that she had turned homely in a few hours, but her expression was not only unfriendly but sour, and her voice was not agreeable. I got out my wallet and extracted my license card. "If you are," I said, "this will identify me," and proffered it.

"Okay, your name's Goodman." She ignored the card. "So what?"

"Not Goodman." I pronounced it again. "Archie Goodwin. I work for Nero Wolfe, who is up in the clubhouse. I just came from there. Why not turn off the radio?"

"I'd rather turn you off," she said bitterly.

Her companion, the redhead who had been with her in the box, reached for the knob, and the radio died. "Look, Lila," she said earnestly, "you're acting like a sap. Invite him in. He may be human. Maybe Bill sent him."

"What did Walt tell us?" Lila snapped at her. "Nero Wolfe is there working with the cops." She came back at me. "Did my husband send you? Prove it."

I bent a knee to put a foot on the edge of the frame, not aggressively. "That's one reason," I said, "why Mr. Wolfe can't stand women. The way they flop around intellectually. I didn't say your husband sent me. He didn't. He couldn't even if he wanted to, because for the past hour he has been kept in the locker room, conversing with a gathering of Homicide hounds, and still is. Mr. Wolfe sent me, but in a way it's a personal problem I've got, and no one but you can help me."

"You've got a personal problem. You have. Take it away."

"I will if you say so, but wait till I tell you. Up to now they have only one reason for picking on your husband. The players left the clubhouse for the field in a bunch, all but one of them. One of them left later and got to the dugout five or six minutes after the others, and it was Bill Moyse. They all agreed on that, and Bill admits it. The cops figure that he had seen or heard something that made him suspect Nick Ferrone of doping the drinks—you know about that? That the Beebright was doped?"

"Yes. Walt Goidell told me."

"And that he stayed behind with Ferrone to put it to him, and Nick got tough and he got tougher, with a baseball bat. That's how the cops figure it, and that's why they're after Bill, as it stands now. But I have a private reason, which I have kept private except for Nero Wolfe, to think that the cops have got it twisted. Mr. Wolfe is inclined to agree with me, but he hasn't told the cops because he has been hired by Chisholm and wants to earn a fat fee. My private slant is that if Bill did kill Ferrone—please note the 'if'—it wasn't because he caught Ferrone doping the drinks, but the other way around. Ferrone caught Bill doping the drinks, and was going to spill it, and Bill killed him."

She was goggling at me. "You have the nerve—" She didn't have the words. "Why, you dirty—"

"Hold it. I'm telling you. This afternoon at the game I was in a box. By the sixth inning I had had plenty of the game and looked around for something to take my mind off it, and I saw an extremely attractive girl. I looked at her some more. I had a feeling that I had seen her before but couldn't place her. The score was eleven to one, and the Giants were flat on their faces, and that lovely specimen was exactly what my eyes needed, except for one flaw. She was having a swell time. Her eyes showed it, her whole face and manner showed it absolutely. She liked what was happening out on the field. There was that against her, but I looked at her anyhow."

She was trying to say something, but I raised my voice a little. "Wait till I tell you. Later, after the game, in the clubhouse, Bill Moyse said his wife was waiting for him, and someone made a crack about showing me her picture. Then it clicked. I remembered seeing a picture of his bride in the Gazette, and it was the girl I had seen in the stands. Again later, I had a chance to ask some of the players some questions, and I learned that she usually drove to games in Bill's light blue Curtis sedan and waited for him after the game. It seemed to me interesting that it made the wife of a Giant happy to see the Giants getting walloped in the deciding game of a World Series, and Mr. Wolfe agreed, but he needed me there in the clubhouse. Finally he sent me to see if she was still around, and here I am. You see our problem. Why were you tickled stiff to see them losing?"

"I wasn't."

"It's perfectly ridiculous," the redhead snorted.

I shook my head. "Rejected. That won't do. Mr. Wolfe accepts my judgment on girls. A pretty girl or a homely girl, a smart girl or a dumb girl, a sad girl or a happy girl— he knows I know. I have told him you were happy. If I go back and report that you flatly deny it, I don't see how he can do anything but tell the cops, and that will be bad. They'll figure that you wanted the Giants to lose because you knew Bill did, and why. Then of course they'll refigure the murder and get a new answer—that Ferrone found out that Bill had doped the drinks, and Bill killed him. They'll start on Bill all over again, and if they—"

"Stop it!" She was hoarse. "For God's sake!"

"I was only saying, if they—"

The redhead put in, leaning to the steering wheel and sticking out her chin. "How dumb can you get?" she demanded.

"It's not a ques—"

"Phooey! You say you know girls! Do you know baseball girls? I'm one! I'm Helen Goidell, Walt's wife. I would have liked to slap Lila this afternoon, sitting there gloating, much as I love her, but I'm not a sap like you! She's not married to the Giants, she's married to Bill! Lew Baker had batted two-thirty-two in the first six games of the series, and he had made two errors and had three bases stolen on him, and still they wouldn't give Bill a chance! Lila had sat through those six games praying to see Bill walk out, and not once! What did she care about the series or the difference between winner's and loser's take? She wanted to see Bill in it! And look at Baker this afternoon! If he had been doped, all right, but Lila didn't know it then! What you know about girls, you nitwit!"

She was blazing. I did not blaze back.

"I'm still willing to learn," I said, not belligerently. "Is she right, Mrs. Moyse?"

"Yes."

"Then I am too, on the main point? You were pleased to see the Giants losing?"

"I said she was right."

"Yeah. Then I've still got a problem. If I accept your version and go and report to Wolfe accordingly, he'll accept it too. Whether you think I know girls or not, he does. So that's some responsibility for me. What if you're a lot smoother and trickier than I think you are? Your husband is suspected of murder, and they're still working on him. What if he's guilty and they could squeeze out of you what they need to hook him? Of course eventually they'll get to you and either squeeze it out or not, but how will I look if they do? That's my problem. Have you any suggestions?"

Lila had none. She wasn't looking at me. She sat with her head lowered, apparently gazing at her hands, which were clasped together.

"You sound almost human," Helen Goidell said.

"That's deceptive," I told her. "I turn it on and off. If I thought she had something Mr. Wolfe could use I'd stop at nothing, even hair-pulling. But at the moment I really don't think she has. I think she's pure and innocent and wholesome. Her husband is another matter. For her sake, I hope he wiggles out of it somehow, but I'm not taking any bets. The cops seem to like him, and I know cops as well as I do girls." I removed my foot from the car frame. "So long, and so forth." I turned to go.

"Wait a minute." It was Lila. I turned back. Her head was up.

"Is this straight?" she asked.

"Is what straight?"

"You're going to tell Mr. Wolfe you're satisfied about me?"

"Well. Satisfied is quite a word. I'm going to tell him I have bought your explanation of your happiness at the game—or rather, Mrs. Goidell's."

"You could be a liar."

"Not only could be, I often am, but not at the moment." She regarded me. "Shake hands with me."

I raised a paw. Her hand was cold, but her grip was firm, and in four seconds our temperatures had equalized. She let go.

"Maybe you can tell me about Bill," she said. "They don't really think he killed Nick Ferrone, do they?"

"They think maybe he did."

"I know he didn't."

"Good for you. But you weren't there, so you don't have a vote."

She nodded. She was being hard and practical. "Are they going to arrest him? Will they really charge him with murder?"

"I can't say. They may have decided while we've been talking. They know the whole town will be rooting for someone to be locked up, and Bill is the leading candidate."

"Then I've got to do something. I wish I knew what he's telling them. Do you know?"

"Only that he's denying he knows anything about it. He says he left the clubhouse after the others had gone because he went back to the locker room to change to other shoes."

She shook her head. "I don't mean that. I mean whether he told them—" She stopped. "No. I know he didn't. He wouldn't. He knows something, and I know it too, about a man trying to fix that game. Only he wouldn't tell, on account of me. I have to go and see someone. Will you come along?"

"To see who?"

"I'll tell you on the way. Will you come?"

"Where to?"

"In the Fifties. Eighth Avenue."

Helen Goidell blurted, "For God's sake, Lila, do you know what you're saying?"

If Lila replied I missed it, for I was on my way around the car. It had taken me no part of a second to decide. This sounded like something. It was a little headstrong to dash off with a damsel, leaving Wolfe up there with mass-production sandwiches, warm beer, and his one measly little fact he was saving up, but this might be really hot.

By the time I got around to the other door Helen had it open and was getting out. Her feet on the ground, she turned to speak.

"I don't want any part of this, Lila. I do not! I wish to God I'd gone with Walt instead of staying with you!"

Lila was trying to get a word in, but Helen wasn't interested. She turned and trotted off toward the gate and the street. I climbed in and pulled the door shut.

"She'll tell Walt," Lila said.

I nodded. "Yeah. But does she know where we're going?"

"No."

"Then let's go."

She started the engine, levered to reverse, and backed the car. "To hell with friends," she said, apparently to herself.

6

Under ordinary circumstances she was probably a pretty good driver, but that night wasn't ordinary for her. As we swung right into 155th Street, there was a little click at my side was we grazed the fender of a stopped car. Rolling up the grade of Coogan's Bluff, we slipped between two taxis, clearing by an inch, and both hackmen yelled at her.

Stopping for a light at the crest, she turned her head and spoke. "It's my Uncle Dan. His name is Gale. He came last night and asked me—"

She fed gas and we shot forward, but a car heading uptown and squeezing the light was suddenly there smack in our path. With a lightning reflex her foot hit the brake, the other car zipped by with at least a foot to spare, she fed gas again, and the Curtis jerked forward.

I asked her, "Taking the West Side Highway?"

"Yes, it's quicker."

"It will be if you make it. Just concentrate on that and let the details wait."

She got to the highway without any actual contact with other vehicles, darted across to the left lane, and stepped on it. The speedometer said fifty-five when she spoke again.

"If I go ahead and tell you, I can't change my mind. He wanted me to persuade Bill to fix the game. He said he'd give us ten thousand dollars. I didn't even want to tell Bill, but he insisted, so I did. I knew what Bill would say—"

She broke off to do some expert weaving, swerving to the middle lane, then on to the right, then a sprint, then swinging to the middle again just ahead of a tan convertible, and so back to the left again in front of a couple of cars that had slowed her down to under fifty.

"Look," I told her, "you could gain up to two minutes this way with luck, but getting stopped and getting a ticket would take at least ten. You're driving—okay, but don't try to talk too. You're not that good. Hold it till we're parked."

She didn't argue, but she held the pace. I twisted around to keep an eye on the rear through the window, and stayed that way clear to Fifty-seventh Street. We rolled down the cobbled ramp and a block south turned left on Fifty-sixth Street, had a green light at Eleventh Avenue, and went through. A little short of Tenth Avenue we turned in to the curb and stopped. Lila reached for the handbrake and gave it a yank.

"Let's hear it," I said. "Enough to go on. Is Uncle Dan a gambler?"

"No." Her face turned to me. "I'm trembling. Look, my hand's trembling. I'm afraid of him."

"Then what is he?"

"He runs a drugstore. He owns it. That's where we're going to see him. I know what Helen thinks—she thinks I should have told, but I couldn't. My father and mother died when I was just a kid, and Uncle Dan has been good to me—as good as he could. If it hadn't been for him I'd have been brought up in an orphans' home. Of course Bill wanted to tell Art Kinney last night, but he didn't on account of me, and that's why he's not telling the cops."

"Maybe he is telling them, or soon will."

She shook her head. "I know Bill. We decided we wouldn't tell, and that settled it. Uncle Dan made me promise we wouldn't tell before he said what he wanted."

I grunted. "Even so he was crowding his luck, telling you two about the program before signing you up. If he explained the idea of doping the Beebright, why—"

"But he didn't! He didn't say how it was to be done, he just said there was an easy way of doing it. He didn't tell us what it was; he didn't get that far, because Bill said nothing doing, as I knew he would."

I eyed her. "You sure of that? He might have told Bill and not you."

"He couldn't. I was there with them all the time. Certainly I'm sure."

"This was last night?"

"Yes."

"What time?"

"Around eight o'clock. We had dinner early with Helen and Walt Goidell, and when we got home Uncle Dan was there waiting for us."

"Where's home?"

"Our apartment on Seventy-ninth Street. He spoke to me alone first, and then insisted I had to ask Bill."

"And Bill turned him down flat?"

"Of course he did!"

"Bill didn't see him alone later?"

"Of course not!"

"All right, don't bite. I need to know. Now what?"

"We're going to see him. We're going to tell him that we have to tell the cops, and we're going to try to get him to come along. That's why I wanted you with me, because I'm afraid of him—I mean I'm afraid he'll talk me out of it. But they've got to know that Bill was asked to fix the game and he wouldn't. If it's hard on Uncle Dan that's too bad, but I can't help it; I'm for Bill. I'm for Bill all the way."

I was making myself look at her, for discipline. I was having the normal male impulses at the sight and sound of a good-looking girl in trouble, and they were worse than normal because I was partly responsible. I had given her the impression that the cops were about set to take her Bill on the big one, which was an exaggeration. I hadn't mentioned that one reason they were keeping him was his recent reactions to the interest Nick Ferrone had shown in her, which of course had no bearing on anyone's attempt to fix a ball game. True, she had been in a mess before I had got to her, but I had shoved her in deeper. What she needed now was understanding and sympathy and comforting, and since her friend Helen had deserted her I was all she had. Which was I, a man or a detective?

Looking at her, I spoke. "Okay," I said, "let's go see Uncle Dan."

The engine was running. She released the handbrake, fed gas, and we rolled. Three minutes got us to Eighth Avenue, where we turned downtown. The dash clock said five past eleven, and my wristwatch agreed. The traffic was heavy in both directions, and she got in the right lane and crawled along. Two blocks down she pulled in at the curb, where there was plenty of space, set the brake, turned off the lights, killed the engine, and removed the key and put it in her bag.

"There it is." She pointed. "Gale's Pharmacy."

It was ten paces down. There were neons in the window, but otherwise it looked drab.

"We'll probably get a ticket for parking," I told her.

She said she didn't care. I got out and held the door, and she joined me on the sidewalk. She put a hand on my arm.

"You're staying right with me," she stated.

"Absolutely," I assured her. "I'm good with uncles."

As we crossed to the entrance and went inside I was

feeling not fully dressed. I have a routine habit of wearing a gun when I'm on a case involving people who may go to extremes, but, as I said, I do not go armed to ball games. However, at first sight of Daniel Gale I did not put him in that category. His drugstore was so narrow that a fat man would have had to squeeze to make the passage between the soda fountain stools and the central showcases, and that made it look long, but it wasn't. Five or six customers were on the stools, and the jerk was busy. A chorus boy was inspecting himself in the mirror of the weight machine. At the cosmetics counter on the other side, the left, a woman was being waited on by a little guy with a pale tight-skinned face and rimless specs who needed a shave.

"That's him," Lila whispered to me.

We stood. Uncle Dan, concentrating on the customer, hadn't seen us. Finally she made her choice and, as he tore off paper to wrap the purchase, his eyes lifted and got Lila. Also he got me, beside her. He froze. He held it, rigid, for four seconds, then came to, went on with the little wrapping job, and was handed a bill by the customer. While he was at the cash register Lila and I crossed to the counter. As he handed the woman her change Lila spoke.

"Uncle Dan, I've got to tell you—"

She stopped because he was gone. Without speaking, he turned and made for the rear and disappeared behind a partition, and a door closed. I didn't like it, but didn't want to start a commotion by hurdling the counter, so I stepped to the end and circled, and on to the door that had closed, and turned the knob. It was locked. There I was, out at first, unless I was prepared to smash the door in.

The soda jerk called, "Hey, Mac, come out of that!"

"It's all right," Lila told him. "I'm his niece. He's my Uncle Dan—I mean Mr. Gale is."

"I never saw you before, lady."

"I never saw you either. How long have you been here?"

"I been here two months, and long enough. Leave me be your uncle, huh? You, Mac, come out here where you belong! Whose uncle are you?"

A couple of the fountain customers gave him his laugh. A man coming in from the street in a hurry approached and called to me, "Gimme some aspirin!" The door I was standing by popped open, and Uncle Dan was there, against me in the close quarters.

"Aspirin!" the man demanded.

"Henry!" Gale called.

"Right here!" the soda jerk called back.

"Wait on the gentleman. Take over for a while; I'll be busy. Come here, Lila, will you?"

Lila moved, circled the end of the counter into the narrow aisle, and approached us. There wasn't room enough to be gallant and let her pass, and I followed Gale through the door into the back room ahead of her. It was small, and the stacks of shipping cartons and other objects took most of what space there was. The rows of shelves were crammed with packaged merchandise, except those along the right wall, which held labeled bottles. Gale stopped near the door, and I went on by, and so did Lila.

"We don't want to be disturbed," Gale said, and bolted the door.

"Why not?" I inquired.

He faced me, and from a distance of five arms' length, with Lila between us, I had my first good view of the eyes behind the specs. I had never seen a pair like them. They not only had no pupils, they had no irises. For a second I thought they were glassies, but obviously he could see, so evidently he had merely been short-changed. Whoever had assembled him had forgotten to color his irises. It didn't make him look any handsomer.

"Because," he was telling me, "this is a private matter. You see, I recognized you, Mr. Goodwin. Your face is not as well known as your employer's, but it has been in the papers on several occasions, and you were in my mind on account of the news. The radio bulletins have included the detail that Nero Wolfe and his assistant were present and engaged by Mr. Chisholm. So when I saw you with my niece I recognized you and realized we should talk privately. But you're an impulsive young man, and for fear you may not like what I say, I make conditions. I shall stay here near the door. You will move to that packing case back of you and sit on it, with your hands in sight and making no unnecessary movements. My niece will put the chair here in front of me and sit on it, facing you, between you and me. That way I will feel free to talk."

I thought he was batty. As a setup against one of my impulses, including a gun if I had had one, it made no sense at all. I backed up to the packing case and lowered myself, resting my hands on my knees to humor him. When Lila saw me complying she moved the chair, the only one there, as directed, and sat with her back to him. He, it appeared, was going to make a phone call. He did touch the phone, which was on a narrow counter at his right under the shelves of bottles, but only to push it aside. Then he picked up a large bottle of colorless liquid, removed the glass stopper, held it to his nose, and sniffed.

"I do not have fainting spells," he said apologetically, "but at the moment I am a little unstrung. Seeing my niece here with you was a real shock for me. I came back here to consider what it might mean, but reached no conclusion. Perhaps you'll explain?"

"Your niece will. Tell him, Lila."

She started to twist around in the chair, but he commanded her, "No, my dear, stay as you were. Face Mr. Goodwin." He took another sniff at the bottle, keeping it in his hand.

She obeyed. "It's Bill," she said. "They're going to arrest him for murder, and they mustn't. They won't, if we tell them how you offered to pay him for fixing the game and he wouldn't do it. He won't tell them on account of me, so we have to. I know I promised you I wouldn't, but now I've got to. You see how it is, Uncle Dan, I've got to. I told Mr. Goodwin, to get him to come along. The best way—"

"You haven't told the police, Lila dear?"

"No. I thought the best way was to come and get you to go with me, and I was afraid to come alone, because I know how bad it will be for you—but it will be worse for Bill if we don't. Don't you see, Uncle—"

"Keep your back turned, Lila. I insist on it. That's right, stay that way." He had been talking in an even low tone, but now it became thin and strained, as though his throat had tightened. "I'll tell why I want your back to me, so I can't see your face. Remember, Goodwin, don't move. This is a bottle of pure sulphuric acid. I was smelling it just to explain why I had it; of course it has no smell. I suppose you know what it will do. This bottle is nearly full, and I'm holding it carefully, because one drop on your skin will

scar you for life. That's why I want your back to me, Lila.
I'm very fond of you—sit still! And I don't want to see your
face if I have to use this acid. If you move, Lila dear, I'll
use it. Or you, Goodwin—especially you. I hope you both
understand?"

Lila was stiff, white, pop-eyed, gazing at me. I may have
been stiff too; anyhow, I didn't move. His hand holding
the bottle was raised, hovering six inches above her head.
She looked as if she might keel over, and I urged her, "Sit
tight, Lila, and for God's sake don't scream."

"Yes," Uncle Dan said approvingly, "I should have
mentioned that. Screaming would be as bad as moving.
I had to tell you about the acid before I discussed matters.
I'm not surprised at your fantastic suggestion, Lila, because
I know how foolish you can be, but I'm surprised at you,
Goodwin. How would you expect me to take a suggestion
that I consent to my complete ruin? When I saw her and
recognized you I knew she must have told you. Of course
you couldn't know what kind of man you had to deal with,
but you know now. Did Lila persuade you that I am an
utter fool, a jellyfish?"

"I guess she must have," I admitted. "What kind of a
man are you?"

He proceeded to tell me, and I proceeded to pretend I
was listening. I also tried to keep my eyes on his pale tight-
skinned face, but that wasn't easy because they were
fascinated by the damn bottle he was holding. Meanwhile
my brain was buzzing. Unless he was plain loony the only
practical purpose of the bottle must be to gain time, and
for what?

". . . and I will," he was saying. "This won't kill you,
Lila dear, but it will be horrible, and I don't want to do it
unless I have to. Only you mustn't think I won't. You don't
really know me very well, because to you I'm just Uncle
Dan. You didn't know that I once had a million dollars
and I was an important man and a dangerous man. There
were people who knew me and feared me, but I was unlucky. I have gambled and made fortunes, and lost them.
That affects a man's nerves. It changes a man's outlook on
life. I borrowed enough money to buy this place, and for
years I worked hard and did well—well enough to pay it
all back, but that was my ruin. I owed nothing and had a

little cash and decided to celebrate by losing a hundred dollars to some old friends—just a hundred dollars—but I didn't lose, I won several thousand. So I went on and lost what I had won, and I lost this place. I don't own this place, my friends do. They are very old friends, and they gave me a chance to get this place back. I'm telling you about this, Lila dear, because I want you to understand. I came to you and Bill with that offer because I had to, and you promised me, you swore you would tell no one. I have been an unlucky man, and sometimes a weak one, but I am never going to be weak again—don't move!"

Lila, who had lifted her head a little, stiffened. I sat gazing at Gale. Obviously he was stalling for time, but what could he expect to happen? It could be only one thing: he expected somebody to come. He expected help. Then he had asked for it, and it was no trick to guess when. As soon as he had seen us he had scooted back here to phone somebody. Help was on the way, and it had to be the kind of help that would deal with Lila and me efficiently and finally; and bigtime gamblers who can provide ten grand to fix a game are just the babies to be ready with that kind of help. In helping with Lila and me they would probably also settle Uncle Dan, since they like to do things right, but that was his lookout, not mine.

Either he was loony or that was it. Doping that was a cinch, but then what? They might come any second; he couldn't be expected to stand and dangle the damn bottle all night; they might be entering the drugstore right now. At a knock on the door he would reach behind him and push the bolt—and here they are. Any second. . .

He was talking. ". . . I didn't think you would, Lila, after all I've done for you. You promised me you wouldn't. Now, of course, you've told Goodwin and it can't be helped. If I just tip this bottle a little, not much—"

"Nuts," I said emphatically, but not raising my voice. "You haven't got it staged right." I had my eyes straight at his specs. "Maybe you don't want to see her face, but the way you've got her, with her back to you, it's no good. What if she suddenly ducked and dived forward? You might get some on her clothes or her feet, but the chair would be in your way. Have you considered that? Better still, what if she suddenly darted sideways in between those cartons? The instant she moved I would be moving too, and that would take her out of my path, and before you could get at her with that stuff I'd be there. She'd be taking a chance, but what the hell, that would be better than sitting there waiting for the next act. Unquestionably it would be better for her to go sideways, with her head down and her arms out. You see how bum your arrangement is? But if you make her turn around facing you—"

She moved. She went sideways, to her left, her head down and her arms out, diving for the cartons.

I lost a tenth of a second because I hadn't dared to pull my feet back ready for the spring, but that was all I lost. I didn't leap, I just went, with all the force my leg muscles could give it. My target was the bottom of the left front leg of the chair, and I went in flat, face down, and had the leg before he could get under way. The impact of the chair knocked him back against the door, and I kept going and grabbed his ankle and jerked. Of course the bottle could have landed right on me, but I had to get him off his feet. As I yanked his ankle I kept my face down, and as he tumbled I felt nothing hit me. The next thing I knew I was on top of him, pinning him, with a grip on his throat, looking around for the bottle. It had never reached the floor. It had landed on a carton six feet to my right and was there on its side, the stuff gurgling out. The floor slanted toward the wall, and no flood threatened me.

"Okay, Lila," I said. "I need help."

She was scrambling to her feet. "Did he—did it—" She giggled.

"No. If you have hysterics I'll tell Bill. Slap yourself, I can't. It's there on a carton, and don't go near it."

"But he—my God, he—"

"Shut up. Company's coming, and we've got to get out of here. I want some adhesive tape, quick. Find some." She moved and started looking on shelves and in drawers. I kept talking, thinking it would help. "A drugstore is a handy place—sulphuric acid, adhesive tape, everything you might need. Watch your step; it's spreading on the floor. When I said I was good with uncles I didn't mean uncles like him. He's a lulu. He may have been—"

"Here it is."

"Good girl. Tear off a piece six inches long—that's it.

No, you'll have to do it; if I turn loose of his throat he'll squawk. Across his mouth, good and tight—not that way, diagonal. That's right. Now one the other way. That ought to do it, thank you, nurse. Now find some nice sterile bandage. . ."

She found that too and held his arms while I sat on his knees and tied his ankles. Then I fastened his wrists behind him and anchored the strip of bandage to the handle of a locked drawer. I squatted for a look at the tape on his mouth, gave it a rub, stood up, went to the door and pushed the bolt, and told her, "Come on."

"But we ought to make—"

"Come on, damn it! If company is on its way, and I think it is, it won't be bottle-danglers. If you like this place you can stay, but I'm going. Well?"

I opened the door, and she passed through. I followed and pulled the door to. There were customers on the fountain stools, though not the same ones, and Henry was selling a man a pack of cigarettes. I paused on my way to the street door to tell him that Mr. Gale would be out soon, then opened the door for Lila. On the sidewalk I told Lila to go wait in the car while I made a phone call. Then I saw she was trembling all over, so I escorted her and got her safely on the front seat.

Up twenty paces was a bar and grill, and I walked to it, entered, found a phone booth, dialed WA 9-8241, asked for Sergeant Purley Stebbins, and got him. He wanted to know if I was up at the Polo Grounds.

I told him no. "Where I am," I said, "is top secret. I'm giving you a hot one. Put this down; Gale's Pharmacy, nine-two-three-two Eighth Avenue. Get a prowl car there fast, and plenty of reinforcements. Gale, the owner, on information received, was the go-between for the gamblers who fixed the ball game. He is in the back room of his store, gagged and tied. The reason—"

"Is this a gag?"

"No. The reas—"

"Where are you?"

"Quit interrupting or I'll ring off. The reason for the hurry is that I think Gale sent for a rescue squad to deal with certain parties who are no longer there, and it would be nice to get there in time to welcome them. So PD cars

should not park in front. Be sure to tell them not to step
in the stuff on the floor that looks like water, because it's
sulphuric acid. That's all. Got the address?"

"Yes, and I want—"

"Sorry, I've got a date. This could make you a lieutenant. Step on it."

I went out and back to the car. Lila was on the driver's
side, gripping the steering wheel with both hands. As I
opened the door her head turned to me.

"Move over," I said. "I'll do the driving this time."

She slid across, and I got in and pulled the door to. I
sat. Half a minute went by.

"Where are we going?" she asked. Her voice was so
low and weak I barely got it.

"Polo Grounds. Where Bill is." Maybe he was.

"Why don't we start?"

"I phoned for cops. If others come before the cops do I
want to get a look at them. In case I forget it later, I want
to mention that that was a beautiful dive you made, and
the timing couldn't have been better. I'm for you—only
spiritual, of course, since you're happily married."

"I want to get away from here. I want to see Bill."

"You will. Relax."

We sat, but not for long. It couldn't have been more
than four minutes before a pair of cops swung around the
corner, headed for the entrance to Gale's Pharmacy, and
entered. Glancing at Lila and seeing that her eyes were
closed, I pushed the starter button.

7

It was only half an hour short of midnight when I stopped
the Curtis at the curb across the street from the main entrance to the Polo Grounds. The mob had dwindled to a
few small knots, and of the long line of police cars only
three were left. Two cops were having a tête-à-tête in front
of the entrance, and another one was leaning against a
wall.

Lila was a quick mover. She had got out and circled
the car to my side by the time I hit the pavement and
shut the door. I gave her the ignition key, and we were

crossing the street when suddenly she let out a squawk and gripped my arm, and then let go and started to run. I took another step and stopped. Bill Moyse was there, emerging from the entrance, with a dick on either side of him and one behind. Lila ended her run in a flying leap and was on him. The startled dicks were on her, or anyway at her. They were vocalizing, and so were Bill and Lila. The two uniformed cops started toward them.

I would have liked to deliver Lila to Wolfe, or at least to Hennessy, but there was a fat chance of tearing her loose from her second-string catcher. Also I did not care to get hung up explaining to a bunch of underlings how I happened to be chauffeuring for Mrs. Moyse, so I detoured around the cluster, made it inside the entrance, and headed for the stairs to the clubhouse. Hearing heavy footsteps above, starting down, and voices, one of them Hennessy's, I slipped quietly to the rear and got behind a pillar. Surely Stebbins had informed the uptown contingent of my phone call about the situation at Gale's Pharmacy, and if so, surely Hennessy would be inquisitive enough to want to take me along wherever he was going. I didn't risk peeking around the pillar, but, judging from the footsteps, there were four or five of them. As soon as they had faded out I returned to the stairs and mounted. I was not chipper. I did not have Lila. I had been gone more than two hours. Wolfe might have gone home. They might all be gone.

But they weren't. Wolfe was in the clubroom, still—or possibly again—on the leather couch, and Chisholm was standing there. As I entered, their heads turned to me.

As I crossed to them Wolfe spoke. "The police are looking for you," he said coldly.

"Uh-huh." I was indifferent. "I just dodged a squad."

"What did you go to that drugstore for?"

I raised the brows. "Oh, you've heard about it?"

"Yes. Mr. Hennessy did, and he was kind enough to tell me." He was dripping sarcasm. "It is a novel experience, learning of your movements through the courtesy of a policeman."

"I was too busy to phone." I glanced at Chisholm. "Maybe I should report privately."

"This is getting to be a goddam farce," Chisholm

growled. His tie was crooked, his eyes were bloodshot, and he had a smear of mustard at the side of his mouth.

"No," Wolfe said—to me, not to Chisholm. "Go ahead. But be brief."

I obeyed. With the training and experience I have had, I can report a day of dialogue practically verbatim; but he had said to be brief, so I condensed it, but included all the essentials. When I finished he was scowling at me.

"Then you don't know whether Gale was actually involved or not. When he failed with Mr. and Mrs. Moyse he may have quit trying."

"I doubt it."

"You could have resolved the doubt. You were sitting on him. Or you could have brought him here."

I might have made three or four cutting remarks if an outsider hadn't been present. I stayed calm. "Maybe I didn't make it clear," I conceded generously. "It was ten to one he had phoned for help—the kind of help that would leave no doubts to resolve—and it might come any second. Not that I was scared, I was too busy, but I wanted to see you once more so I could resign. I resign."

"Bosh." Wolfe put his hands on the leather seat for leverage and raised himself to his feet. "Very well. I'll have to try it." He moved.

Chisholm put in, "Inspector Hennessy said to notify him immediately if Goodwin showed up."

Wolfe wheeled on him, snarling. "Am I working for you? Yes! By heaven, I am! Notify Mr. Hennessy? Hah!" He turned and strode through the door that led to Art Kinney's office.

"It's a farce," Chisholm muttered and followed him.

I fell in behind.

They were all in there. The four who were famous athletes, first-string Giants, didn't look very athletic. Their sap had started draining with the first inning of that awful ball game, and it hadn't stopped for more than ten hours. Lew Baker, catcher, and Con Prentiss, shortstop, were perched on a desk. Joe Eston, third baseman, and Nat Neill, center fielder, were on chairs.

Art Kinney, manager, was standing over by a window. Doc Soffer was seated at Kinney's desk, bent over, with his elbows on his knees and his face covered by his hands.

Beaky Durkin was propped against a table, saggy and bleary-eyed.

"It had better be good," someone said—I didn't know who, because I was placing a chair for Wolfe where he could see them all without spraining his neck. When he was in it, with nothing to spare between the arms, I crossed to a vacant seat over by the radio. Chisholm was there, at my right.

Wolfe's head moved from side to side and back again. "I hope," he said grumpily, "you're not expecting too much."

"I'm through expecting," Kinney muttered.

Wolfe nodded. "I know how you feel, Mr. Kinney. All of you. You are weary and low in spirit. You have been personally and professionally humiliated. You have all been talked at too much. I'm sorry I have to prolong it, but I had to wait until the police were gone. Also, since I have no evidence, I had to let them complete their elaborate and skilled routine in search of some. They got none. Actually they have nothing but a druggist that Mr. Goodwin got for them."

"They've got Bill Moyse," Con Prentiss rumbled.

"Yes, but on suspicion, not on evidence. Of course I admit, because I must, that I am in the same fix. I too have a suspicion but no evidence, only mine is better grounded. I suspect one of you eight men of drugging the drinks and killing Ferrone. What I—"

They made enough noise to stop him. He showed them a palm.

"If you please, gentlemen. I have a question to put. I suspect one of you, but I have no evidence and no way of getting any speedily. That is why I asked Mr. Chisholm to keep you here for consultation with me after the departure of the police. I wanted to ask you: do you want to help? I would like to tell you the reason for my suspicion and ask you to help me get evidence to support it. I think you can if you will. Well?"

"One of us?" Joe Eston demanded.

It was interesting to see them. Naturally they all had an impulse—anyhow, all but one—to look around at faces, but no two of them handled it exactly alike. Chisholm looked straight and full at each in turn. Beaky Durkin sent quick little glances here and there. Doc Soffer, frowning and pursing his lips, turned his head slowly left to right.

"Go ahead, damn it!" Kinney blurted. "Have you got something or not?"

"Yes, I have something," Wolfe assured him, "but I don't know how good it is. Without your help it is no good at all."

"We'll help if we can. Let's hear it."

"Well. First the background. Were the two events—the drugging of the drinks and the murder—connected? The reasonable supposition is yes, until and unless it is contradicted. If they were connected, how? Did Ferrone drug the drinks, and did one of his teammates discover it and, enraged, go for him with the bat? It seems unlikely." Wolfe focused on Beaky Durkin. "Mr. Durkin, most of what you told me has been corroborated by others, but you knew Ferrone better than anyone else. You discovered him and got him here. You were his roommate and counselor. You told me that because of his brilliant performance this season his salary for next year would be doubled; that his heart was set on winning today's game and the series; that winning or losing meant a difference of some two thousand dollars to him personally; that his series money would pay his debts with some to spare; and that, knowing him intimately, you are positive that he could not have been bribed to drug the drinks. Is that correct?"

"It sure is." Durkin was hoarse and cleared his throat. "Nick was a swell kid." He looked around as if ready for an argument, but nobody started one.

"I know," Wolfe said, "that the police got no impeachment of that. Do any of you dispute it?"

They didn't.

"Then, without evidence, it is idiotic to assume that he drugged the drinks. The alternative, supposing that the two events were connected, is the reverse—that someone drugged the drinks and Ferrone knew or suspected it and was going to expose him, and was killed. That is how I see it. Call him X. X could have—"

"To hell with X," Kinney blurted. "Name him!"

"Presently. X could have put the drugged drinks in the cooler any time during the late morning, as opportunity offered. What led Ferrone to suspect him of skulduggery may not be known, but conjecture offers a wide choice.

Ferrone's suspicion may have been only superficial, but to X any suspicion whatever was a mortal menace, knowing as he did what was going to happen on the ball field. When Ferrone questioned him he had to act. The two were of course in this room together, at the time the rest of you were leaving the clubroom for the field or shortly after. X was, as so many have been, the victim of progressive exigency. At first he needed only money, and to get it he stooped to scoundrelism; but it betrayed him into needing the life of a fellow man."

"Cut the rhetoric," Chisholm snapped. "Name him."

Wolfe nodded. "Naming him is easy. But it is pointless to name him, and may even expose me to an action for slander, unless I so expound it as to enlist your help. As I said, I have no evidence. All I have is a fact about one of you, a fact known to all of you and to the police, which seems to me to point to guilt, but I admit that other interpretations are conceivable. You are better judges of that than I am, and I'm going to present it for your consideration. How can I best do that?"

He aimed his gaze at Baker and Prentiss, who were perched on a desk, raised a hand slowly, and scratched the tip of his nose. His eyes moved to pin Doc Soffer. His head jerked to the left to focus on Chisholm, and then to the right, to Beaky Durkin.

He spoke. "I'll illustrate my meaning. Take you, Mr. Durkin. You have accounted for yourself, but you have been neither contradicted nor corroborated. You say you left the clubhouse shortly before the team did and went to your seat in the grandstand."

"That's right." Durkin was still hoarse. "And I didn't kill Nick."

"I didn't say you did. I am merely expounding. You say you remained in your seat, watching the game, until the third inning, when you were sent for by Mr. Chisholm to come to the clubhouse. That too is neither contradicted nor corroborated. Certainly you were there when you were sent for, but there is no proof that you had been there continuously since the game started and even before."

"I don't know about proof, but I was. I can probably find the guy that was sitting next to me."

"You didn't leave your seat once during that time?"

"I did not."

Wolfe looked around. "Well, gentlemen. That's the fact I can't explain. Can you?"

They were gawking at him. "Do we have to?" Baker demanded.

"Someone does." Wolfe's voice sharpened. "Consider the situation. Consider the relationship of those two men. The discovery of Ferrone is Durkin's proudest achievement as a baseball scout. He fosters him and treasures him. Today—now yesterday—at the game that will be the climax of Ferrone's triumphant season, Durkin is in the clubroom and sees Ferrone there in uniform, with the others, young, sound, mighty, valiant. He leaves the clubhouse and goes to a seat in the grandstand, and soon he sees the team cross the field to the dugout, but no Ferrone. Durkin keeps his seat. Before long the loudspeaker announces that Garth, not Ferrone, will play second base. Durkin keeps his seat. The players take the field, and the game starts, with no Ferrone. Durkin keeps his seat. They play the first inning badly. Durkin keeps his seat. They play the second inning badly. Durkin keeps—"

"Good God!" Art Kinney yelled, moving.

"Exactly." Wolfe lifted a hand. "Please, gentlemen, keep your seats. It is clearly fantastic. The announcement that Garth would play second base could have been taken by Durkin merely as a blunder, but when they took the field without Ferrone his disquiet and consternation would have been insupportable. The one thing he couldn't possibly have done was to stay in his seat. Why did you, Mr. Durkin?"

"I couldn't think—" He tried to clear his throat and sounded as if he were choking. "There was nothing I could do. What could I do?"

"I don't know. I said I can't explain what you did do, but I can try. Suppose the nonappearance of Ferrone was no surprise to you, because you knew where he was and what had happened to him. Suppose, further, you were in a state of severe systemic shock because you had murdered him. I submit that that explanation of your keeping your seat is plausible. Is any other? Can you offer one?"

Durkin took two steps. "Look here," he said, "you can't sit there and accuse me of a thing like that. I don't have to stay here and take it, that kind of thing. I don't have to, and I'm not going to."

He started for the door, but Lew Baker was suddenly there in his path and speaking. "Back up, Beaky. I said back up!"

Beaky did so, literally. He backed until his rump hit the edge of the table, and felt for the edge with his hands, one on each side, and gripped it.

Wolfe was grim. "I was supposing, Mr. Durkin, not accusing. But I am now ready to accuse, and I do. I explained, when I was calling you X, how and why you acted." His eyes moved. "Gentlemen, I ask you to look at him. Look at his face, his eyes. Look at his hands, clutching the table in dismay and despair. Yes, I accuse him. I say that that man drugged your drinks, caused you to lose your game, and, threatened with exposure, murdered your teammate."

They were making sounds, and they were on their feet, including Art Kinney.

"Wait!" Wolfe said sharply, and they turned to him. "I must warn you, you approach him at your peril, for I have no proof. It will be gratifying to crush him, to press a confession out of him, but a confession is not evidence, and we need some. I suggest that you try for it. He did it for money, and surely he was paid something in advance, unless he is pure fool. Where is it? Certainly not on his person, since you have all been searched, but it is somewhere, and it would do admirably. Where is it?"

Lew Baker got to him ahead of the others. He told him in a thin, tight voice, so tight it twanged, "I wouldn't want to touch you, Beaky, you dirty rat. Where is it? Where's the jack?"

"Lew, I swear to God—"

"Skip it. You swearing to God! You fixed us, did you? And Nick—you fixed him. I'd hate to touch you, but if I do, God help you!"

The others were there, Kinney and Doc Soffer with them, crowding in on Durkin, who had pulled back onto the table, still gripping the edge. I went to the end of the table and stood. They were strong and hard, and their nervous systems had had a tough day. Aside from the killing of Nick Ferrone, whom they may or may not have loved, this was the bird who had made them play ball like half-witted apes in the most important game of their lives, to an audience of fifty million. If they really cut loose there could be another corpse in that room.

"Give me room, fellows," Nat Neill said. "I'm going to plug him."

Durkin didn't flinch. His jaw was quivering, and his eyes looked sick, but he didn't flinch.

"This is wrong," Con Prentiss said. "He wants us to hurt him. He'd like to be knocked cold. He's not a coward, he's just a snake. Did you see his eyes when you said you'd plug him? That's what he wants."

"It's a moral question," Joe Eston said. "That's the way to handle it; it's a moral question."

Art Kinney shouldered between two of them to get his face within ten inches of Durkin's. "Look, Beaky. You've been in baseball thirty years. You know everybody in the majors, and we know you. What do you think's going to happen? Where could you light? We've got you here now, and we're going to keep you. I'll send for the whole damn team. How will you like that?"

"I want a lawyer," Durkin said in a sudden burst.

"By God!" Neill roared. "He wants a lawyer! Get out of the way! I'm going to clip him!"

"No, Beaky, no lawyers," Kinney said. "I'll send for the boys, and we'll lock the doors. Where's the money? We know you got it. Where is it?"

Durkin's head went forward, down. Kinney put a fist under his chin and yanked it up and held it. "No, you don't. Look at me. We've got you, but even if we didn't, where could you go? Where you going to sleep and eat? You're done, Beaky. Where's the money?"

"Let me hold his chin," Neill requested. "I'll fix his goddam chin."

"Shut up," Eston told him. "It's a moral question."

Kinney's fist was still propping Durkin's chin. "I think," he said, "the boys ought to have a look at you. They won't be sleeping anyhow, not tonight. Con, get on the phone and find them. You too, Lew—the one in the clubroom. Get 'em here, and get all of 'em you can. They'll come all right. Tell them not to spill it; we don't want any cops around until we get—"

"No!" Durkin squawked.

"No what, Beaky?" Kinney removed his fist.

"I didn't mean to kill Nick." He was slobbering. "I swear I didn't, Art. He suspected—he asked me—he found out I bet a grand against us, and he threw it at me, and I brought him in here to explain, but he wouldn't believe me and he was going to tell you, and he got sore and came at me, and I grabbed the bat just to stop him, and when I saw he was dead—my God, Art, I didn't want to kill Nick!"

"You got more than a grand for doping the drinks. How much did you get?"

"I'm coming clean, Art. You can check me, and I'm coming clean. I got five grand, and I've got five more coming. I had to have it, Art, because the bookies had me down and I was sunk. I was listed good if I didn't come through. I had it on me, but with the cops coming I knew we'd be frisked, so I ditched it. You can see I'm coming clean, Art. I ditched it there in the radio."

"What radio?"

"There in the corner. I stuffed it in through a slot."

There was a scramble and a race. Prentiss tangled with a chair and went down with it, sprawling. Nat Neill won. He jerked the radio around and started clawing at the back, but the panel was screwed on.

"Here," I said, "I've got a—"

He hauled off and swung with his bare fist, getting his plug out of his system, though not on Durkin. Grabbing an edge of the hole his fist had made, he yanked, and half the panel came. He looked inside and started to stick his hand in, but I shouldered him good and hard and sent him sideways. The others were there, three of them, surrounding me. "We don't touch it, huh?" I instructed them, and bent down for a look in the radio, and there it was, lodged between a pair of tubes.

"Well?" Wolfe called as I straightened up.

"A good fat roll," I told him and the world. "The one on the outside is a C. Do you—"

Beaky Durkin, left to himself on the table, suddenly moved fast. He was on his feet and streaking for the door. Joe Eston, who had claimed it was a moral issue, leaped for him as if he had been a blazing line drive trying to get by, got to him in two bounds, and landed with his right. Durkin went down all the way, slamming the floor with his head, and lay still.

"That will do," Wolfe said, as one who had earned the right to command. "Thank you, gentlemen. I needed help. Archie, get Mr. Hennessy."

I went to Kinney's desk and reached for the phone. At the instant my fingers touched it, it rang. So instead of dialing I lifted it and, feeling cocky, told it, "Nero Wolfe's uptown office, Archie Goodwin speaking."

"That you, Goodwin?"

I said yes.

"This is Inspector Hennessy. Is Durkin there?"

I said yes.

"Fine. Hold him, and hold him good. We cracked Gale, and he spilled his guts. Durkin is it. Gale got to him and bought him. You'll get credit for getting Gale, and that'll be all right, but I'll appreciate it if you'll hold off and let it be announced officially. We'll be there for Durkin in five minutes. Hold him good."

"We're already holding him good. He's stretched out on the floor. Mr. Wolfe hung it on him. Also we have found a roll of lettuce he cached in the radio."

Hennessy laughed. "You're an awful liar, Goodwin. But you're a privileged character tonight, I admit that. Have your fun. We'll be there in five minutes."

I hung up and turned to Wolfe. "That was Hennessy. They broke Gale, and he unloaded. He gave them Durkin, and they're coming for him. Hennessy doesn't believe we already got him, but of course on that we've got witnesses. The trouble is this: which of us crossed the plate first— you with your one little fact, or me with my druggist? You can't deny that Hennessy's call came before I started to dial. How can we settle it?"

We can't. That was months ago, and it's not settled yet.

ABOUT THE AUTHOR

REX STOUT, the creator of Nero Wolfe, was born in Noblesville, Indiana, in 1886, the sixth of nine children of John and Lucetta Todhunter Stout, both Quakers. Shortly after his birth, the family moved to Wakarusa, Kansas. He was educated in a country school, but, by the age of nine, was recognized throughout the state as a prodigy in arithmetic. Mr. Stout briefly attended the University of Kansas, but left to enlist in the Navy, and spent the next two years as a warrant officer on board President Theodore Roosevelt's yacht. When he left the Navy in 1908, Rex Stout began to write freelance articles, worked as a sightseeing guide and as an itinerant bookkeeper. Later he devised and implemented a school banking system which was installed in four hundred cities and towns throughout the country. In 1927 Mr. Stout retired from the world of finance and, with the proceeds of his banking scheme, left for Paris to write serious fiction. He wrote three novels that received favorable reviews before turning to detective fiction. His first Nero Wolfe novel, *Fer-de-Lance*, appeared in 1934. It was followed by many others, among them, *Too Many Cooks, The Silent Speaker, If Death Ever Slept, The Doorbell Rang* and *Please Pass the Guilt*, which established Nero Wolfe as a leading character on a par with Erle Stanley Gardner's famous protagonist, Perry Mason. During World War II, Rex Stout waged a personal campaign against Nazism as chairman of the War Writers' Board, master of ceremonies of the radio program "Speaking of Liberty" and as a member of several national committees. After the war, he turned his attention to mobilizing public opinion against the wartime use of thermonuclear devices, was an active leader in the Authors' Guild and resumed writing his Nero Wolfe novels. All together, his Nero Wolfe novels have been translated into twenty-two languages and have sold more than forty-five million copies. Rex Stout died in 1975 at the age of eighty-eight. A month before his death, he published his forty-sixth Nero Wolfe novel, *A Family Affair*.

REX STOUT
&
NERO WOLFE

Rex Stout created Nero Wolfe, that Falstaff in girth and wit, that serious eater, devoted orchidologist and acknowledged agoraphobe. Nero solves crimes by sheer brain-power and with more than a little help from the brash but efficient Archie Goodwin.

Nero Wolfe made his dazzling debut in 1934, when his creator was forty-seven years of age. Since then the 286-pound, sedentary sleuth has triumphed over a variety of evil forces that have even included the F.B.I. Wolfe accomplishes these feats between beers in a brownstone on West 35th Street in New York. Dispensing with crime laboratories and the like, he relied on old-fashioned logic of the sort practiced by Sherlock Holmes (the vowels in whose name are identical to Nero Wolfe's, even in their order).

Mr. Stout's Nero Wolfe books have appeared in over twenty-two languages and have sold more than forty-five million copies. Mr. Stout had completed forty-six mysteries starring Wolfe at the time of his death at eighty-eight. The first was *Fer-de-Lance,* the last *A Family Affair*. In between, there were forty-four other mysteries, each one of them a brilliant display of the talents of Rex Stout and the expert sleuth Nero Wolfe.

Bantam is currently bringing back into print one Rex Stout mystery each month. They are available wherever paperbacks are sold.

WHODUNIT?

Bantam did! By bringing you these masterful tales of
murder, suspense and mystery!

Bantam Book Catalog

Here's your up-to-the-minute listing of over 1,400 titles by your favorite authors.

This illustrated, large format catalog gives a description of each title. For your convenience, it is divided into categories in fiction and non-fiction—gothics, science fiction, westerns, mysteries, cookbooks, mysticism and occult, biographies, history, family living, health, psychology, art.

So don't delay—take advantage of this special opportunity to increase your reading pleasure.

Just send us your name and address and 50¢ (to help defray postage and handling costs).